KV-370-617

VIRGINIA REEDE

Witch's
KNIGHT

ELLORA'S CAVE
ROMANTICA PUBLISHING

*W*hat the critics are saying...

ဆ

"Witch's Knight is a wonderful adventure...that kept me turning the pages with pleasure as I read." ~ *Just Erotic Romance Reviews*

. "Virginia Reede creates a story filled with swashbuckling action, deception, and unbridled lust." ~ *Ecataromance Reviews*

"A fast-moving story, chock full of hot, steamy sex." ~ *The Romance Studio*

"Fans of the historical with strong paranormal elements ...will love this one." ~ *Love Romances*

"A magical adventure full of sexual escapades, mystical mysteries and personal growth." ~ *Fallen Angel Reviews*

"The heat that sizzles in Witch's Knight will keep the reader warm until the dawn." ~ *Erotic Escapades*

An Ellora's Cave Romantica Publication

www.ellorascave.com

Witch's Knight

ISBN 9781419956683
ALL RIGHTS RESERVED.
Witch's Knight Copyright© 2005 Virginia Reede
Edited by Kelli Kwiatkowski
Cover art by Syneca

Electronic book Publication November 2005
Trade paperback Publication June 2007

This book is printed in the U.S.A. by Jasmine-Jade
Enterprises, LLC.

With the exception of quotes used in reviews, this book may
not be reproduced or used in whole or in part by any means
existing without written permission from the publisher,
Ellora's Cave Publishing, Inc.® 1056 Home Avenue, Akron OH
44310-3502.

This book is a work of fiction and any resemblance to persons,
living or dead, or places, events or locales is purely
coincidental. The characters are productions of the authors'
imagination and used fictitiously.

Content Advisory:

S – ENSUOUS
E – ROTIC
X – TREME

Ellora's Cave Publishing offers three levels of Romantica™ reading entertainment: S (S-ensuous), E (E-rotic), and X (X-treme).

The following material contains graphic sexual content meant for mature readers. This story has been rated E–rotic.

S-*ensuous* love scenes are explicit and leave nothing to the imagination.

E-*rotic* love scenes are explicit, leave nothing to the imagination, and are high in volume per the overall word count. E-rated titles might contain material that some readers find objectionable — in other words, almost anything goes, sexually. E-rated titles are the most graphic titles we carry in terms of both sexual language and descriptiveness in these works of literature.

X-*treme* titles differ from E-rated titles only in plot premise and storyline execution. Stories designated with the letter X tend to contain difficult or controversial subject matter not for the faint of heart.

Also by Virginia Reede

ഇ

Beastmistress
Men in Chains (Cerridwen Press)

About the Author

ഇ

Virginia welcomes comments from readers. You can find her website and email address on her author bio page at www.ellorascave.com or www.cerridwenpress.com.

Tell Us What You Think

We appreciate hearing reader opinions about our books. You can email us at Comments@EllorasCave.com.

WITCH'S KNIGHT

ဆာ

Chapter One

ઠ૭

Geoffrey was lost.

He reined in his horse and surveyed the clearing for any sign of a path. If there had ever been one, a lush growth of spring grasses and flowers now obscured it. The three knights who were Geoffrey's escort drew abreast.

"Nice to be out of the wood," commented Wilfred. He inhaled deeply. "Beautiful here."

"It would be a sight more beautiful if I could find the road." Even as he grumbled, Geoffrey could not help but notice Wilfred was right. The meadow stretched before them like a shallow bowl, ringed by the forest walls. He breathed deeply, expanding his lungs. The heady scents of wildflowers and fresh air were wonderful after the dank forest. But there was something odd about this meadow. Its borders were too sharply delineated to be natural. Why would such an enormous clearing sit in the middle of a wood, seemingly uninhabited, even by ruins?

"The road is probably just grown over," said Wilfred, interrupting Geoffrey's musings. "If we just look at the edge of the field where it led out of the trees, we should be able to pick it up." The four men turned their horses and faced the direction from which they had come. As one, their countenances clouded in confusion.

"I do not see the opening." Geoffrey voiced the thought in all their minds. He scanned the line of trees. They appeared to be too close together to accommodate even a single horse and rider, yet they had all ridden through a wide passage only moments before. Or had they?

"It is a trick of the light. We are looking from the wrong angle." The tone of Horace's voice belied his confident words, and Geoffrey realized his escort was sharing the strange feeling of unease that had invaded his own thoughts.

"You are no doubt right, Horace." Geoffrey made sure his own voice did not hold any trace of misgiving. As the group's leader, he could not afford to display uncertainty. "We'll just follow our own tracks back to the trees…" Geoffrey trailed off, his brow furrowed in puzzlement as he looked at the ground at their horses' feet. Four mounted men, even as lightly armored as they were, should have left a clear trail of trampled grasses. Instead, the floor of the meadow seemed undisturbed.

"What kind of plants are these?" Geoffrey dismounted and examined the ground near his horse's hooves. Flowers, clover, even the delicate ferns—all seemed undisturbed. He took a few experimental steps, deliberately placing his feet on the more fragile-looking plants. When he turned to retrace his footsteps, everything had sprung back into place, leaving no evidence of his passage.

Geoffrey glanced up at Wilfred, whose quizzical look indicated he had not missed the significance of Geoffrey's performance. "Perhaps," he said slowly, his eyes on Wilfred's, "we should head back toward where we think we rode out of the trees and scout up and down for the road."

"Or we could ride over to the opposite side of the meadow," suggested Horace, "and try to find where it picks up again."

Geoffrey shook his head. "We do not know that it does pick up again." Seeing the alarm on the knights' faces, he continued, "I am not saying it does not pass through this meadow. If we go back to where the road left the wood, we can pick it up again and follow more carefully this time. If it ends at the meadow, we will know we were given bad directions, and we can turn around and head back to that last village."

10

Groans erupted at the suggestion of retracing the long route through the dim and airless forest, but none of the knights would have thought to contradict Geoffrey. He remounted his horse and turned to face the direction from which they had come, then hesitated. Where had they entered? They had emerged from the trees at the highest point of the shallow depression that contained the clearing, but from his current position, Geoffrey was no longer sure. Realizing his hesitation was doing nothing to quell his men's growing unease, he started resolutely toward the dark green wall.

By the time Geoffrey reached the ring of trees, his uncertainly had magnified. He could discern no gap large enough to admit a horseman. Nevertheless, he turned and walked his horse slowly along the meadow's border, hoping some trick of the light concealed the opening. He could hear the comments of his men becoming less frequent before dying entirely. They rode in silence, with no sound other than the whispers of the horses' hooves against the springy, green carpet. When the tension became so thick he could no longer ignore it, Geoffrey halted.

"We must have gotten turned around in the field," he said. "We will go back the other way." Without comment, the troop turned and repeated the process in the opposite direction. As Geoffrey's sense of unease threatened to bloom into outright panic, he desperately considered what his next suggestion must be. The responsibility of leading the knights— especially the young Horace, who was making his first true errand on his king's behalf—weighed heavily upon him.

Geoffrey led the troop along the impenetrable barrier until it became obvious they were heading downhill. Knowing this was wrong he called a halt and turned toward the group of followers. Forcing a smile, he said, "Well, it appears your leader must admit his sense of direction is less than perfect. Let us dismount and stretch for a few minutes, and I am sure I will regain my bearings."

Wilfred chuckled, causing Geoffrey to bless him silently. By far the most experienced knight still riding in the service of the king, this grizzled warrior could do more to calm the nerves of the younger men with a single word — or laugh — than Geoffrey himself. As the group slid from their saddles to stretch, the two youngest wandering off to relieve themselves in the tall grass, Wilfred followed Geoffrey to where he had bent on one knee.

"What do you plan to do next?" he asked the leader without preamble. "Even if we do find the road, the day grows long. I would not like to be in the middle of this wood when darkness falls."

"Aye, neither would I." Again, Geoffrey scanned the sunlit clearing. "We could make camp here, I suppose."

Wilfred considered. "We could," he said slowly, "but I do not know what explanation we would give for doing so. And..."

"And what?" Geoffrey was unaccustomed to hearing doubt in Wilfred's voice.

"There is something...unnatural about this meadow. I am not a superstitious man, but I am not sure I would want to close my eyes in such a place."

Standing, Geoffrey glanced over Wilfred's shoulder to make sure the other men were still too far away to overhear. "I feel it, too. But I do not know what other choice we have. We could continue searching the edge of the trees, but if we do not find the way out by nightfall — "

"If there is a way out," Wilfred interrupted flatly, voicing the fear that had been growing in Geoffrey's mind. He was, if possible, even less credulous than Wilfred, but a nagging idea had formed, and he could no longer ignore it.

"Wilfred, I am beginning to think this place is under some sort of enchantment." Geoffrey more than half expected Wilfred to scoff at this suggestion, but the old knight's face remained grave.

"Considering the nature of our errand, it is not surprising such thoughts should enter our minds," replied Wilfred.

Geoffrey nodded. Only he and Wilfred knew the true motive behind the king's request, and Geoffrey was now glad he had not shared this information with the less experienced members of the group. Noticing the other two wandering back toward them, he made a decision. "Stay here with the others, Wilfred. You can regale them with some of your tall tales, and prevent them from becoming even more nervous. I am going to pick up where we left off searching, on foot this time. If I do not find something in an hour, we will make camp." Wilfred grunted his assent, and Geoffrey turned again toward the dense fence of foliage that was beginning to look like the wall of a prison.

Geoffrey continued on his downhill path along the edge of the field, turning after a time to gauge the distance he had come. He realized the contours of the ground were not as smooth as they had previously appeared. Gentle folds hid all but the tops of the men's heads, and as the slope continued to dip, his view of the troop was completely obscured by the gently waving grasses.

After a few moments, Geoffrey began to hear something over the buzz of bees and twitter of birds. It was the sound of running water, which he found greatly encouraging. At least if they had to camp, they need not be thirsty. Following his ears, Geoffrey soon came upon a small stream that flowed out of the forest and ran noisily through a shallow depression between two small rises.

Geoffrey examined the break in the trees that marked the brook's entry into the glade. "Not as wide as where we came in," he mused aloud, "but a man might be able to lead a horse through, if we can find no other way."

"I would not recommend it," replied a voice, startling Geoffrey to the roots of his hair. Automatically, he drew his sword and whirled to face the speaker. Every muscle and nerve was on full alert, and he felt the familiar tingle that always presaged a confrontation.

Geoffrey was accustomed to instantly intimidating those he thus faced, both with his size and with the fluid grace with which he wielded his sword. Instead, the face he confronted wore an expression of mild amusement.

Eyes so green they seemed to mirror the color of the spring grass looked boldly into Geoffrey's own. "I am sorry I startled you," came a voice that was soft without a trace of timidity, "but I hardly think I deserve to be," the speaker glanced down, "penetrated."

Geoffrey's eyes followed her glance, and he saw that the tip of his sword rested against the pale rise of two exceptionally voluptuous breasts. Instantly, he withdrew its point and relaxed his position.

"Forgive me, lady," said Geoffrey, for despite her simple clothing, the woman he faced was obviously well born, "but I did not see you before, or hear you draw near." A slight inclination of the lady's head acknowledged and accepted his apology, and he went on. "Where did you come from, that you were hidden from view?"

"From farther down the valley," she replied. "I could see you, but my eyes are accustomed to the ways of this place." Geoffrey waited for her to say more, but she only continued to regard him as if she found him vastly entertaining. Growing uncomfortable with both her silence and her gaze, he spoke again.

"I was looking for the road. My men and I," Geoffrey gestured in the direction where he believed his men waited, "seem to have gotten turned around."

"I guessed as much." Again, Geoffrey was surprised when she did not continue, and felt compelled to speak.

"Can you show me where the road enters the meadow? I was unable to locate where we came in."

"Certainly," said the creature, tilting her head slightly to the side so that her strawberry curls caught the light breeze. "But would you not rather continue toward your destination than go back through the forest?"

"Our destination?" Geoffrey was puzzled. This woman spoke as if she knew exactly where he was headed. This was, of course, impossible, but he could not shake his initial impression.

"It would not appear you are out for an afternoon's ride to enjoy the spring weather," came her dry rejoinder. "The road through the meadow ends only a short distance beyond, at the village. I assume you are headed there."

"If the village is called Caernham, we are. And I would greatly appreciate your assistance if you could point us in the right direction."

The woman looked at him speculatively. "The people of Caernham are shy of visitors, and might not be pleased if I were to lead four armed knights to their doors."

"We mean them no harm," said Geoffrey. He realized that in his confusion, he had forgotten his manners. "Forgive me, lady, but I have not introduced myself. I am Sir Geoffrey, and my knights and I are on an errand for the king."

"And that errand takes you to Caernham?" To Geoffrey's surprise, the young woman seemed unimpressed by the mention of the king, and had not even paused before posing her question. "A tiny village that only farms and keeps a few sheep seems unlikely to contain anything of interest to King Liam."

"What we seek is not actually in the village," Geoffrey explained, "but we were told the villagers might have information that would help us." It occurred to him this woman might be able to answer the very question he planned to pose to the villagers. "Perhaps you can enlighten me, and save me from having to disturb them."

"If I can, I will be happy to."

"Then, my lady, perhaps you have heard of the witch of Caernathen. Can you tell us how to find her?"

"The witch of Caernathen?" Her amusement seemed to grow. "I have not heard that particular appellation."

"But you know of a witch who lives in the Caernathen wood? She is reputed to be very powerful."

"Oh, it was not 'Caernathen' that surprised me. It was the word 'witch'. The local people do not use it."

Geoffrey was becoming frustrated by their conversation. It seemed this woman was deftly avoiding giving a direct answer to any of his questions.

"Witch, sorceress…I do not care what she is called. There is a woman who practices magic and is said to be very able at spells and foretelling. I do not believe in such things myself, but the king does, and he has sent me to speak with this…person."

"I see." The woman seemed to consider, then make up her mind. "Very well. I will take you and your men where you wish to go, and we need not travel through the village and alarm everyone. I will wait here while you gather your men."

Now it was Geoffrey's turn to consider. After his experience with the vanishing road, he was reluctant to let his guide out of his sight. She seemed to read his mind.

"Do not worry, I will not disappear." As if to emphasize her statement, she seated herself on a large rock next to the stream. Geoffrey inclined his head to her, and started to hurry off. He was stopped by her voice.

"Sir Geoffrey!"

He turned to find her smiling broadly. "That way." She pointed, indicating a direction almost opposite that in which he had started. Deciding it would be better to trust her sense of direction than his own, he altered his course, and almost immediately heard the voices of his men and the quiet sounds of the resting horses.

The men were surprised and delighted to learn Geoffrey had found a local who would lead them out of the meadow. They quickly mounted and followed their leader down the gentle slope.

As they neared the stream, Geoffrey was much relieved to see the afternoon sun glinting on red-gold hair. He would have been most embarrassed if he had again set out in the wrong direction. The lady rose to greet them, and Geoffrey realized that while he had introduced himself, she had not done the same.

"Forgive me, my lady, but I do not know your name, and I would introduce you to my men."

"My name?" Her mouth curved in a mischievous smile. "But you have brought me a new one. I am Leonore. Also known, apparently, as the witch of Caernathen."

Chapter Two

ಐ

The cottage's main room was surprisingly large and the air within it clear of smoke, despite the merry fire that danced in the hearth. The room glowed with light from beeswax candles. Geoffrey had seen such things before, but only on the king's table, and then only during special celebrations. They emitted a pure light and a sweet scent.

"They are made here."

"I beg your pardon?" Geoffrey was startled by Leonore's voice.

"The candles. The villagers make them. Caernham is renowned for its bees." She gestured toward the candles and smiled. "You seemed interested in them."

"Yes." After Leonore's revelation in the meadow, Geoffrey still found himself somewhat at a loss for words. "They are very fine." Geoffrey looked around and realized his knights looked even more uncomfortable than he felt. All were unmarried—Wilfred had little use for women, and Horace and Morgun had barely entered manhood. More accustomed to inns and stables than cozy rooms, they did not seem to know whether to sit or stand.

His thoughts were interrupted by the appearance of a plump young woman. She carried a tray of carved wooden goblets and began placing them on a long table at one end of the room.

"Dinner will be ready in just a bit, my lady," she said. "You were right about the number of guests?"

"Yes, Cortlyn. Will they have time for a bath?" At the young girl's assent, Leonore turned to Geoffrey. "Besides our bees, we are also blessed by hot water that bubble out of the earth. After your long ride, I am sure you and your men would enjoy relaxing in the spa."

Geoffrey was so astonished by this suggestion that he did not immediately reply. To his surprise, Wilfred spoke. "Do you mean a Roman spa? With bathing pools and a hypocaust?"

"Our water comes to us already hot," said Leonore, smiling at the old knight. "And the pools are mostly natural, but they were enlarged by someone long ago, probably the Romans."

"I have not seen a real Roman bathing pool since I was a young man and traveled to the old fort at Cumbria." Wilfred glanced self-consciously at Geoffrey, and then turned his attention back to Leonore. "For my part, I would accept your most generous offer." To Geoffrey's amazement, Wilfred made a small but courtly bow.

"I hope you will all accept it. Will you not follow me?" Leonore turned and exited through a side door, followed eagerly by a grinning Wilfred. The two younger knights looked uncertain, but when Geoffrey nodded, they reluctantly followed. Geoffrey almost ran into the three men as he stepped over the threshold, bowing his head to avoid the lintel. All had stopped in their tracks, and Geoffrey saw why.

As the last light of the day was about to fade, the three-quarter moon rose above the horizon—enormous and yellow—and seemed close enough to touch. It was reflected in two dark, round pools from which steam curled in eerie wisps, like ghosts dancing on their mirrored surfaces. A tiny waterfall fell from one end of the upper pool into a lower one, which narrowed into a stream that ran under one end of the house. Fallen blossoms from an overhanging tree floated on the lower pool's surface and perfumed the air.

Low stone benches surrounded both baths, and a wooden frame stretched over the upper pool, making an insubstantial roof through which stars glimmered. A heavy cloth, like those used for making sails, was folded at one end, and Geoffrey could see rope handles that could be used to pull it over the frame to make a shelter. He felt they had wandered into a dream, and Leonore's low laugh did little to break the illusion.

"I will leave you to your baths," said Leonore. "I have a few matters to attend to, if we are to leave in the morning. Please spend as long as you wish—Cortlyn has prepared a stew, and 'twill only improve as it simmers."

The moment Leonore disappeared into the cottage, Wilfred began stripping off his gear and clothing and soon stood naked, gingerly testing the upper pool's water temperature with one foot. A grin slashed through his gray and red beard and, heaving an enormous sigh of satisfaction, he sank quickly up to his neck in the steaming pool. "Come on in, lads. 'Tis grand!"

Geoffrey and the two younger knights followed more slowly, until all were seated on benches built into the side of the pool so that the water covered their shoulders. On the small estate that Geoffrey oversaw for the king, there was a house that contained a bathing tub, but heating the water necessary to fill it was a tedious task and he had only managed to bathe in it on a very few occasions. Also, the tub was not large enough to have one's entire body immersed. This pool seemed large enough to accommodate ten men, and the lower pool was even larger.

As they all began to relax, Horace voiced what had been on all of their minds since Leonore's startling revelation in the forest meadow. "Do you really think she is a witch? I thought they were all crones. She is young and beautiful."

"Maybe she is old and ugly," suggested Morgun, "and she is using some kind of spell to appear as she does." Wilfred snorted in derision at this idea, but Geoffrey considered the idea carefully. A day ago—even a few hours ago—he would have said he did not believe in witches, especially those with the ability to change their appearance. But the odd incident in the meadow was still unexplained, and there was also this...feeling. Geoffrey tried to put it into words, but failed. He just did not feel things here were normal.

In any case, he could not imagine Leonore as "old and ugly". While she was not beautiful in the stiff, carefully coiffed and gowned manner of the most admired noblewomen of Liam's court, she had a different kind of beauty. She had an earthy, loin-stirring quality that was at once natural and otherworldly. Geoffrey's groin had tightened every time she spoke. And when she turned those grass-green eyes on him, brimming with amusement—

"Excuse me," came a quiet voice, interrupting Geoffrey's thoughts. He looked up to see a young man laden with a large wooden box. "Leonore thought you might like something to wash with." He set down the box and began removing square cakes of soap and a large jar of what looked like honey. "This is for washing your hair," he explained, probably in reaction to the knights' mystified expressions.

"I was hoping it was honey mead," said Wilfred. "It looks too good to pour on my head."

"Oh, I'll be bringing you some wine as well," the young man hastened to add. "I just could not carry it all at once." He continued to remove items from the box, including some soft brushes with wooden handles and small cloths, presumably for washing. Finally, he removed some larger cloths, which he placed on one of the stone benches. "You can dry off with these when you are ready to get out. If you would like your clothes cleaned, I can bring you something to wear."

Geoffrey was about to refuse when Wilfred spoke up. "I was just thinking what a shame it would be to put these travel-soiled garments on my fine, scrubbed body."

Meanwhile, Horace investigated the substance in the jar and added, "Not to mention how much your old clothes stink. You will smell so pretty after using this stuff your horse will think a woman is riding him." Despite his teasing words, Horace was already spreading the honey-thick liquid on his head and rubbing it into a lather.

"Please tell the lady it is very kind of her to offer, but it is really not necessary to go to any extra trouble for us," Geoffrey told the serving man, if that is what he was. He did not carry himself like a servant. Neither, for that matter, had Cortlyn, now that he considered it.

"It is no trouble," said the young man. "Leonore was expecting you, and asked Cortlyn and me to come and help for the evening. I have everything prepared, and it will not take a moment." He picked up his box and headed back around the side of the house.

"She knew we were coming, did she?" said Wilfred. He was energetically scrubbing his back with one of the long-handled brushes and continuing to smile broadly. "Maybe she really is a witch."

"And she spoke of leaving with us in the morning," said Geoffrey, "although I will swear none of us mentioned the king's orders were to bring her back with us."

They were all mulling this over when the man reappeared with his box, on which he was carefully balancing a large stone jar. This time, the box held several carved wooden cups, laid on top of four carefully folded garments.

"They look like cassocks," remarked Geoffrey as they were removed from the box and draped across a stone bench.

"But made of much softer stuff," assured the young man, as he tilted the contents of the jar first into one cup and then another. He passed them around to the men then set the jar where it could easily be reached from the pool. He then gathered up their discarded clothes and boots, leaving their swords and all else behind. "If you need anything else before dinner, just call out. My name is Dunfred." With that, he returned to the house, leaving the men to their bath and drink.

After the first sip from his cup, Wilfred proclaimed, "Well, whatever she is, she serves a good wine." He moved over nearer to Geoffrey and clapped him on the back. "Relax, young sir, and enjoy your good fortune. When you have been a soldier as long as I, you will know to take your pleasure when you are lucky enough to get it." Without spilling a drop of his wine, Wilfred dunked his head under and came up, water streaming down his face, to take another sip from the cup. "Besides, anyone who provides me with a bath like this is a lady by my reckoning."

"A lady she is indeed," agreed Geoffrey. "By her manner of speech if nothing else. But what is a highborn lady doing living alone in a wood in the middle of nowhere?"

* * * * *

Seated on benches at the long table, the men soon lost their self-consciousness over their unaccustomed attire and bare feet. The meal was unusual as well. Geoffrey had often eaten a midday meal in the king's hall, where trenchers were divided and pewter goblets shared, and courses served in a carefully prescribed manner. He had also eaten much smaller evening meals at inns, where everything was piled into a single bowl and designed to be more filling than enjoyable.

Here, each diner had a wooden plate and goblet, and food was placed in bowls and platters in the center of the table. They served themselves with large spoons provided for that purpose. And what food! Leonore's reference to "stew" had hardly prepared Geoffrey for the savory concoction of pork, herbs and vegetables, which Cortlyn explained should be spooned over the soft mixture of grains that sat alongside.

Geoffrey had been surprised to see Dunfred and Cortlyn take seats on the long benches. Leonore sat at the chair on one end of the table and Geoffrey was at the other end, as she had directed. More of the excellent wine was served, and the group had become quite merry. Even Morgun, usually too shy to speak in groups, was chatting volubly with Dunfred about the lands he expected to take over on the king's behalf on his next birthday.

Although Geoffrey appreciated being placed at the head of the table, he found himself feeling somewhat jealous of

Wilfred and Horace, with their close proximity to Leonore. *She really is beautiful.* The thought sprang unbidden into his mind for perhaps the tenth time since the meal had begun. Her green eyes sparkled wickedly and her white teeth flashed in the candlelight as she laughed at something Wilfred said. *I thought the old dog did not care for women,* he thought sourly to himself. *He is flirting like a smitten schoolboy.*

Leonore raised her goblet to her lips, which Geoffrey could not help but notice were full and almost as red as the wine. She sipped it and said something conspiratorial to Morgun, who blushed scarlet in the candlelight. Wilfred, who had apparently overheard the joke, laughed uproariously. Geoffrey had suddenly had enough of the meal. The warmth from the sweet-scented fire, the wine and the sparkle of the candles were starting to make his head spin. He rose from his seat.

"My lady, as excellent as both this meal and the company have been, I think we knights must see to our horses and be off to a good night's sleep if we are to ride in the morning. His Majesty is eager for our return, and I want to leave as early as possible." Muffled groans arose from the younger knights, but a glance from Geoffrey silenced them.

"Your horses have already been tended," replied Leonore, setting down her goblet, "but I am sure you will want to see for yourself. Beds have been prepared for each of you, and your gear has already been taken to your rooms."

"Thank you. Wilfred?" The two younger knights had already risen to their feet, but Wilfred was still seated, holding a goblet in one hand and a partially eaten pastry in the other. After only the briefest hesitation, he put both down and stood.

Leonore spoke again. "Dunfred will show you to the stables and then to your room. If you do not mind, Sir Geoffrey, I would speak with you alone after you have satisfied yourself the arrangements are acceptable." Geoffrey nodded his agreement, and Dunfred rose to lead the way.

Geoffrey found the horses snugly housed in a spacious shed not far from the bathing pools and next to a tidy croft. Satisfied, he allowed the group to be taken back to the cottage, where exterior stairs led to a sleeping loft. Here, three thick straw mattresses had been placed on the floor, covered by beautiful woven blankets. Everything looked very clean and the men, who had anticipated a night sleeping on the ground, were well pleased.

"There are only three beds," said Geoffrey, "and my gear is not here."

"Leonore asked us to prepare three beds in the loft, and to bring your gear to her. I do not know what she did with it." Dunfred seemed unconcerned.

"Never mind, I was going down to speak with her anyway." Dunfred left, and Geoffrey turned to his men. "She must have assumed I would prefer my own chamber. If I do not return tonight, I will call you at first light."

Geoffrey found Leonore seated next to the fire in a tall chair. Seeing him, she indicated the seat opposite. "I wanted to thank you again for your hospitality. We did not expect a night of leisure and luxury when we set out on our quest."

"I was happy to do it," Leonore replied easily. "Will you have more wine?" She indicated a jar and goblet on the small table next to his chair, and Geoffrey noticed for the first time that she too held a goblet. Although he was still feeling the effects of the wine he had consumed in the bath and at dinner, he poured himself a small quantity, thinking it would make the ensuing conversation easier.

"I need to ask you some questions, my lady." Geoffrey's tone was cautious—he was not sure how to begin.

"Please, call me Leonore."

"Ah. Yes. Well, Leonore, I gather you already know of the reason for our errand."

"I probably know less than you think," she replied. "I had a…I suppose you would call it a vision, that I must go on a journey, and four men, led by someone who…by someone like yourself would take me there. Since I had no plans for travel, I knew you would be coming here to find me. When you said you were on an errand for the king, I assumed he had sent for me. Was I correct?"

"Yes," said Geoffrey, feeling somewhat dazzled. The firelight made her skin glow and turned her red hair to a deep copper. He was again struck that her beauty was somehow otherworldly, and Geoffrey's sense of unreality was only enhanced by the matter-of-fact way she spoke of her 'vision'. He did not know how he felt about it, but he had no other explanation for the fact she had begun preparations for his arrival many hours in advance. There was no other way she could have known, was there?

Geoffrey tried to concentrate. Had they spoken aloud of their errand in one of the villages through which they had passed? Could someone have ridden ahead and warned her? It did not seem likely, but Geoffrey was still not ready to concede the gorgeous creature before him had supernatural powers.

"You are willing to come with us, then?" he asked her, although she had already implied this.

"Of course," replied Leonore. "He is my king. But before you take me before him, I should tell you I have no idea why the king should want to see me. It would be most unfortunate for you take me to stand before him, only to learn I do not have the skill to do what he asks."

"I see." Geoffrey took another sip of the excellent wine, trying to decide if there was any reason not to reveal the king's plight. It was not likely to remain a secret for long, in any case, and she would have to be told eventually.

"Someone has kidnapped his son, Wesley."

"The Crown Prince?" Leonore looked dismayed. The handsome young prince was very popular with the people of the kingdom, and her concern seemed genuine. "Who?"

"Therein lies the problem. We do not know who has done this thing, but the circumstances lead the king to believe it must be one of his close allies. Several had the opportunity, but to accuse the wrong one would be disastrous politically."

"I can see that, yes." Leonore looked into the fire meditatively. "And the king believes I could divine the culprit?"

"Yes, and perhaps even help recover his son before anyone finds out the kidnapping has taken place. Although the guilty party may find a way to make the news public, if it serves his ends."

"Hmmmm." Leonore considered this. "I may be able to help, especially if he was taken by force."

"Why do you say that?" asked Geoffrey. Leonore looked up as if realizing she had spoken thoughts aloud.

"If he was taken by force, he was probably frightened or at least angry. Strong emotions sometimes leave sort of a…a footprint, as it were. Sometimes I can see it and get a sense of what the person who had those emotions heard or saw."

"Like the face of the person who took him?"

"Like that. Or other things. Each time is quite different, and I may learn nothing of value. But chances will be best if I can be taken to the place where it happened."

"We are not sure about that, but we have some ideas."

She nodded. "Good. It is a place to start." She returned her stare to the fire, no doubt considering the task ahead. Geoffrey was about to excuse himself when he remembered he did not know where to go.

"Oh, I almost forgot to ask. Dunfred said he took my things to you, and only three beds were made up in the loft. Where am I to sleep tonight?"

Leonore's eyebrows rose and an especially pretty smile curved her full lips. "With me, of course."

Chapter Three

≈

Leonore could not help but enjoy Geoffrey's discomfort. It was obvious he did not believe in what he would doubtless refer to as "magic" or "sorcery". Every time a reference to her abilities was made, his face went blank. He was plainly trying not to offend her while keeping his skepticism intact.

But Geoffrey learning that she intended for him to share her bed was the best moment by far. Leonore had known he would be shocked. She had anticipated his reaction, and now savored it. He was barely managing to keep his mouth from hanging open. It was delicious, and it increased her desire for him.

He probably thinks he has successfully hidden his attraction to me. Leonore loved and admired men of strong principles, even if some of those principles were based in meaningless conventionality. *Such as the idea that a true lady would never invite a man she has known for less than a day into her bed.* Leonore suppressed a chuckle. This was going to be fun.

"I-I am sorry, but I do not think I understood you correctly." Geoffrey, his cheeks darkened with a flush, stuttered.

He is even more handsome when he is flustered. The combination of jet-black hair and bright blue eyes had arrested Leonore from the first moment she saw him. His chiseled features, however, held more than a touch of arrogance. Leonore was wickedly delighted to see him in a situation he did not immediately know how to handle. She was sure it was not something to which he was accustomed, and it softened him in a way that was most pleasing.

"I told you I had a vision of your arrival," she began. When Geoffrey, watching her with great intensity, nodded, she continued. "I knew the leader of the group I was expecting would become my lover." The truth was more complicated, but Leonore was enjoying the impact of her words too much to muddy the water with details.

"You knew that the...that I..." Geoffrey swallowed visibly and tried again. "That we would become..."

"Lovers," Leonore repeated. "And since it is a foregone conclusion, I see no reason why we should wait. Once I am occupied with the king's dilemma, we may have few opportunities. Do you not agree?"

"I suppose," said Geoffrey, confusion plain on his face.

Poor man, I should have prevented him from drinking so much wine. "Of course, I may be making a false assumption. You *do* wish to make love with me, do you not? Or do you find me unattractive?"

"Yes! No!" Geoffrey looked out of breath. "I mean yes, of course I find you attractive. Beautiful, in fact. I just am not used to...I usually do not..."

"You usually do not find yourself being invited to bed by a woman who does not make such matters her profession," Leonore finished for him. "I am sure this is unusual for you, but that is no reason we should not," Leonore ran her eyes slowly along Geoffrey's long and muscular frame, "enjoy one another while we can."

Geoffrey opened his mouth as if to answer and then shut it again. The confusion on his face gave way to wonder and, finally, a smile.

"You agree, then?" asked Leonore, matching his smile with one of her own.

"I would be a fool not to."

"Excellent." Leonore set down her wine goblet and stood, and Geoffrey hastened to do the same. "Shall we go?" She held out her hand to him and, after a moment's hesitation, he took it. She led him through the one door that she had kept closed since her guests' arrival. Surreptitiously, she watched his face so she could enjoy his reaction to what lay beyond. His expression was all she could have wished. Illuminated by candles she had lit before seating herself by the fire was the chamber that held her bed.

Leonore knew it was unlikely Geoffrey had ever seen so large a bed unless, perhaps, he had ever had occasion to enter the king's bedchamber. King Liam's bed was legendary for its size—as was the king himself. A bed with a raised wooden frame, however, was rare even among the wealthy.

The bed had been an indulgence. A carpenter had been in Leonore's debt, and had offered to build her any piece of furniture she desired. She had designed the bed to her own glorious specifications, and he had made it for her with hands that held both the skill of a master craftsman and the talent of an artist. At Leonore's behest, a skilled weaver from the village had collaborated with a seamstress to make a mattress grand enough to befit such a beautiful bed, and the two had gone on to design bedding and cushions to delight both the eye and the touch. The two women swore they had enjoyed their commission so much they almost refused payment, but Leonore had insisted.

Leonore loved her extravagant bed, and had been anticipating the moment she would share it with Geoffrey since she had laid eyes on him. Her vision had promised her a remarkable lover, but she had not known until his arrival that he would be pleasing to both the eye and the mind. Now the time had come to fulfill the first part of the prophecy her vision had revealed.

Leonore closed the door behind them and, standing at the foot of the bed, turned to face Geoffrey. She reached up with one hand and smoothed back the black curls from his high, smooth forehead. He, in turn, caught her hand and brought it to his mouth. Turning it over, he pressed his lips against the palm, all the while staring into her eyes with that intense blue gaze. She felt a ripple of desire run through her body, ending with a delightful tingle in her nether regions.

Never breaking her gaze, Leonore put her other hand on the center of Geoffrey's chest and ran it lightly across the light growth of soft hair that was scattered over his hardened muscles. She pushed the loose robe off one of his shoulders then ran her hand down to where it was belted. She pulled the fabric loose so the garment fell down around his waist, exposing his entire chest. Retrieving her hand, she placed her lips on the hollow just above his breastbone and forced his chin back as she kissed, licked and nibbled up his throat and along the line of his jaw. She felt him shudder as a low groan escaped him.

Geoffrey's head turned and his mouth found hers. Frissons of delight trembled through her nerves as she delighted in the taste and feel of his tongue—still flavored with the sweet wine—against her own. She sucked it for a few moments then teased it with her own tongue, taking her turn to taste his lips and the inside of his mouth. She pressed her body against his and felt the ridge of hardness that pressed between them.

Her head began to swim. *What is happening?* She knew well the art of mutual seduction—to torment and be tormented until the moment of release. Leonore had always been firmly in control—even when she let herself walk the precipice of abandon, only her body fell, never her mind.

But the moment she felt Geoffrey's hard shaft pressing against her belly, her body squeezed and shuddered with an urgency that threatened to engulf her. *Take me! Fill me!* With a tremendous effort of will, Leonore pulled her lips from Geoffrey's and opened her eyes to stare at him, panting with desire.

His eyes looked glazed and his hands reached for the front of her kirtle. Eager to help, she stepped back and unfastened the girdle that held it in place, then guided his hands as he pulled the outer garment over her head. She watched as his eyes fell to the breasts she knew he could see molded through the thin fabric of her smock. He reached out and grasped them through the gossamer covering, and she felt another jolt of pleasure as his thumbs brushed her already-erect nipples.

He fumbled for the ties that held the front of her smock together, and she reached around and grasped his firm buttocks through the cassock, pressing their lower bodies closer together even as she leaned back to give him access to the ribbons he was trying to unlace without tearing. He groaned as she pulled him hard against her and, seemingly giving up on the laces, pulled the front of her smock apart so suddenly, the final two ties snapped and her breasts spilled out into his waiting hands.

"Now look what you have done," she said. She had intended for her tone to be teasing, but her voice came out ragged. *Who is this man? Why does he affect me so?* Taking a deep breath, she endeavored to keep her tone light before continuing, "Cortlyn will have to repair them for me, and I do not know how I will explain—"

Before Leonore could finish her sentence, Geoffrey leaned forward to move his mouth toward her breasts, and her voice was cut off in a rush of breath as the shift in weight forced her back onto the soft mattress. He took one nipple gently between his teeth and began teasing it with his tongue, and she moaned as waves of heat shot through her limbs. She closed her eyes and threw her head back against the silky covers. He tasted first one breast and then the other, suckling and licking as if he was drawing sustenance from them.

As shudders raced through her, Leonore placed her hands on his shoulders and pushed him back so she could climb the rest of the way out of her ruined undergarment. Running his eyes hungrily up and down her naked body, Geoffrey attempted to climb onto the bed after her, only to be hampered by the robe that was still tied around his waist with the loosened sash. He pulled the offending garment the rest of the way off and let it fall to the floor.

"Wait!" Geoffrey froze at Leonore's tone and looked at her as if alarmed. Little did he know that she was struggling for control. "Let me take a moment to look at you," she said, and he relaxed slightly. Leonore forced herself to take a long leisurely look at his body, fully revealed at the height of his excitement.

"No woman has ever looked at me as you do," he said.

"No? Then the women you have known are fools. You are magnificent." And he was. His legs were long and muscular, and his rampant cock thrust forward below his hard stomach. A fine line of dark hair ran from the dark growth at his groin up his belly and spread like the branches of a tree along the clearly defined muscles of his chest. His face was almost as beautiful as a woman's, but with a hardness that could never be mistaken for anything but masculine. Her eyes again fell to his engorged shaft, and Leonore imagined feeling its silky hardness in her hands, between her lips, within her body. She could wait no longer to touch him.

"Come to me," she commanded, and he did not hesitate. Immediately, his long body was poised above hers, then he lowered his head and she felt his face against the tender skin of her belly. His beard, rough without being unpleasant, tickled the sensitive places above her groin as his tongue lapped against her navel.

"You are the one who is magnificent," he breathed, as his hands slid beneath her buttocks and lifted her sex, causing her thighs to fall open. She felt him pause, and looked down to see his eyes close as he seemed to breathe in the scent of the red curls. "You have bathed yourself with something that smells like springtime, but your own scent is like summer." So saying, he plunged his face into the coppery depths of soft hair, and she felt the hot wetness of his tongue trace between the swell of her lips and catch gently against the hood that surrounded the bud at their joining.

So unexpected was his skill that she bucked and almost jerked her body off the bed at the sudden sensation that washed through her limbs. "Oh, Geoffrey, I take back what I said about the women you have known," she gasped. "Someone has taught you very well indeed."

Geoffrey continued his ministrations to her throbbing bud, and Leonore thought she must scream in pleasure. He lifted his head and grinned at her. "You taste better than the honeyed fruit at your table tonight. I could do this all night."

"If you do, I may die of ecstasy before morning."

"We cannot allow that," he replied in a mock-serious tone. "King Liam would be most annoyed with me."

"As will I if you do not come up here," she said, putting her hands under his arms and trying to pull him upward. He complied, and again Leonore found her mouth being devoured. She could taste her own muskiness on his lips and face, and found herself aroused by the knowledge that he had tasted her so deeply. She reached between their bodies and found his shaft, hot and harder than iron. *If it was any hotter, it would burn my hand.*

Geoffrey groaned as she grasped his cock tightly, running her thumb across the silky skin at its tip. She could feel the indentation around the opening and teased it with her thumbnail. When a tiny drop of liquid formed, she smoothed it into the skin of the shaft. A thought flashed through her mind. *I need to go slowly, or I will be lost.*

With her other hand she reached down and touched her own sex, moaning when she found it wet and swollen from his attentions. With her fingers, she parted its lips and guided the head of his cock to its entrance. Without releasing her grasp on the shaft, she lifted her hips so her outer lips surrounded only the tip, then pushed ever-so slightly so she could begin to feel her inner muscles grasp the widest part of the head. She squeezed simultaneously with her hand and her body, and felt his answering shudder.

"I can wait no longer," breathed Leonore. "Please…" Releasing his manhood, she grasped his hips and guided him so he slid a little farther inside her, stopping him again as her body tightened around him. Little by little, she pulled him forward until their bodies met and he could go no further. For a few moments they lay still, her body grasping and compressing as his throbbed and pulsed.

Now, it was Geoffrey's turn to control the pace. Leonore thought she must explode as he began to slide slowly in and out of her, slick with her juices and as hot as a glowing brand. "Ah, Sir Knight, you will burn me with your fire!"

"Then let us pound out the flames." With an inarticulate cry, Geoffrey quickened his rhythm and Leonore rose to meet him. Moment by moment, they went faster and faster, as he pulled back and drove deep. Leonore's body expanded and contracted, and the fire in her belly spread out in a mounting wave. She lost all sense of where she was or the other guests in the house, as her gasps became louder and turned to screams as each thrust forced another exclamation of pleasure from her body. "Geoffrey!" she shrieked, and she was just barely aware that he called her name as well.

All the heat, all the fire, all the waves coalesced into a single, tangible orb of pleasure that contracted fiercely into a fist-sized mass of power. Suddenly, magic filled the air around her. It was drawn from the very Earth by the inexorable pull of her ecstasy. *Wait*, she thought dimly, *I did not call for you. How did you…*

An orgasm tore through Leonore, stopping all questions. Magic flooded into her and she was barely able to prevent it from rushing through the center of her body and into Geoffrey. She had not felt so out of control in years. Wave after wave flashed through her — magic and pleasure, pleasure and magic. And still the fiery brand of Geoffrey's cock slammed into her, while his shouted name turned to inarticulate gasps as she shuddered and bucked, riding the wave of power and pleasure that joined them so that each became indistinguishable from the other.

Abruptly, the thrusts stopped and his back arched away from her. Leonore opened her eyes and saw Geoffrey's face contorted in soundless ecstasy. She forced herself to be still and was rewarded by the deep pulsing sensation as his hot seed pumped into her willing loins. She lay back, forcing herself to savor the moment as she waited for her heartbeat to slow and her breathing to regulate. "Thank you, Geoffrey. Thank you." She sighed, searching her mind for her accustomed control. It was there—barely. *I almost lost my…what? My self?*

Geoffrey rolled from her and lay on his back amid the jumble of cushions and bedclothes. "I do not think any woman has after thanked me after…after that."

"Well, they should have." Leonore propped herself up on one elbow and looked at him. "Especially if that was a typical performance."

Geoffrey grinned from his pillow. "Maybe not typical. I could have done better had I not enjoyed so much of your excellent wine."

"Better than that?" Leonore feigned incredulity. "Sir Knight, you make a simple country girl's heart weak at the very thought."

Geoffrey laughed aloud. "I have not yet decided what you are, Leonore, but I am quite sure you are no simple country girl."

"Perhaps not," Leonore conceded. "But it was not sexual pleasure alone I thanked you for. It was the renewal of my power."

"I beg your pardon?" Geoffrey eyed Leonore suspiciously.

"Yes, well, although I do not generally refer to myself as a witch, I do have certain abilities somewhat beyond those of other people. But in order to use them, I must have an inner source. And feeling the way you just made me feel strengthens that source."

"You are saying you must *couple* in order to do magic?" Geoffrey's eyebrows rose in a skeptical expression.

"No—at least not for everyday magic. But if I am going to do something especially challenging, yes, I need a certain amount of sexual gratification to be at my best." She smiled sweetly into his astonished face. "I feel ready to do just about anything right at the moment."

"What do you mean by 'everyday magic'?"

"Oh, soothing someone's headache or predicting the weather," she replied. "The little things I do to help the local people, or to make my days more pleasant."

"Can you do this any time you wish?" Geoffrey drew himself to a sitting position and faced her.

"The simpler things, I can. Like anything else, repetition makes it easier. It is the things I do less often, such as healing a serious injury or," she smiled, "finding a missing prince that takes extra strength. My vision told me I would be going on a journey that would take me to a task that would require great strength, and the person leading that journey would be able to provide all the strength I needed." Actually, it had told her a great deal more than that. Something about it had been troubling, but she had not yet figured it out for herself, and would certainly not speak of it to another.

Geoffrey's eyes clouded and his brows drew together ominously. "Are you saying you only asked me into your bed to be…to be fuel for your fire?"

"Not at all." Leonore chose her words carefully. This man's pride was obvious, and she did not want to insult him. "I would never have a man in my bed I was not attracted to, for any reason. My vision would not have revealed you as my lover if you were not someone for whom I would feel desire." She looked at his still-beetled brows. Obviously, he did not know whether he should be offended. Although she enjoyed teasing Geoffrey, it would not be helpful for them to be at odds.

"I must tell you that you exceeded my highest expectations in every way. When I saw you in the meadow, I was delighted at your physical appearance. But by the end of dinner, having had the opportunity to speak with you and watch you with your men, I assure you I was entirely smitten. And now having made love with you…" Leonore shrugged elegantly, as if the conclusion was obvious.

"That is flattering, Leonore," replied Geoffrey slowly, still looking cautious, "but how can you know me well enough to be 'smitten', as you put it, in the course of one evening?"

"It is given to me the ability to look into men's minds sometimes." At the alarmed look on Geoffrey's face, she hastened to continue. "Only if bidden or if extreme need arises. I have not violated your innermost thoughts, nor would I. But it is impossible for me to be unaware of the general tone of someone's mind. Yours is clear and straightforward, without the shadows caused by deception. Your men have complete confidence in you. This tells me a great deal about the kind of man you are." *As did my vision*, she did not add.

"I see." Geoffrey still did not look happy, but he seemed at least temporarily satisfied with her explanation. "I suppose if a man finds himself in a comfortable bed with a beautiful woman, he should not ask too many questions." He grinned. "Especially when he has just been very thoroughly satisfied by that very woman."

"I think I am the one who was satisfied," said Leonore, pleased the conversation was turning again to a more pleasant subject. "But do not tell me you are sated! There are many hours before we must ready ourselves for our journey, and I do not plan to spend all of them sleeping." So saying, she reached for Geoffrey again, and was rewarded by a bawdy laugh.

Chapter Four

ॐ

Everything about the day was entirely too normal. The morning was cool and overcast and the forest no longer seemed like an impenetrable maze of trees, but an ordinary wood with an ordinary trail. The horses were well rested and calm, and if the men were a little cleaner than one would normally expect on the return leg of a middle-sized journey, they had fallen into their accustomed banter and riding order. Except for the extra horse and rider, everything was exactly as it should be.

Geoffrey heard a musical laugh, and willed himself not to turn around and see which of the men had amused Leonore. He had expected she would ride at his side when the trail permitted, but since the march had started, she had flitted from the front to the back of the line like a hummingbird on the nimble horse she rode as if it was an extension of her own limbs. She had ridden next to him, but had paid no more attention to him than she had to any of the others. Geoffrey was not sure why this annoyed him so much.

When he had awakened in Leonore's bed this morning, he had been alone. Disappointment had quickly given way to apprehension as he heard the sound of others stirring. A pale light was already beginning to glow outside the unshuttered window. Had it been open the night before? Had the entire household heard the sounds of their passion? Naked, he looked around and was relieved to find his clothes hanging from a peg. Had they been there last night or had Dunfred or, even worse, Cortlyn brought them in while he lay sprawled naked across the bedclothes?

Geoffrey had thought to speak with Leonore privately before he had to confront his men. He felt it was better if they

39

behaved as if no particular intimacies had taken place between them, at least for the time being. Now he would have to walk out of her bedroom into…what?

Steeling himself, he entered the main room, relieved to see that although the long table held platters of bread and cold meats, no one was seated and the sounds seemed to come from the kitchen, which was around a corner. He headed in that direction and almost collided with Cortlyn, who was carrying a steaming kettle that smelled of fragrant herbs.

"Good morning, Sir Geoffrey. Leonore has gone to tell your men the food is ready." Geoffrey detected nothing unusual in her face or tone, and nodded before heading out to the back. He met Horace and Morgun returning from the stable.

"Where is Wilfred?" he asked, after they greeted him.

"He is getting dressed," replied Horace, grinning. "He got up early to have one last bath before we left."

"And a fine thing it was." Geoffrey looked up to see Wilfred coming down the outdoor stairs from the sleeping loft. "Good morning, sir. I hope your sleeping accommodations were as comfortable as ours?"

Geoffrey surveyed Wilfred's face for any hidden meaning, but could detect nothing. The old soldier's hair was wet and his face was rosy and scrubbed. He smelled strongly of the honey-scented soap. It was oddly disconcerting to detect the same aroma that had perfumed Leonore's hair wafting from this grizzled and masculine form. Geoffrey quickly turned away.

"There is food and tea ready," he said.

"Aye, Lady Leonore told us," said Morgun, blushing. Apparently, he could not even mention her name without reacting. "She is putting some more things into her horse's pack." Geoffrey nodded as if this was of no particular interest and led them into the house.

Leonore had not joined them for the short breakfast, stopping in only to say she needed to inventory her herbs, in case any might be helpful in her task for the king. As she disappeared into the kitchen, Geoffrey found himself seated next to Cortlyn and Dunfred. They were discussing closing up the house after the group's departure and returning to their homes in the village. At the mention of two homes, Geoffrey was surprised.

"You do not live together? I assumed you were…"

"Married? Not yet." Dunfred spoke as Cortlyn blushed prettily. "We are to be married this month. It has been a long wait."

"Why did you have to wait?" Geoffrey was curious.

"Leonore had need of Dunfred," said Cortlyn. "She said she would no longer require his help, so we are to be married as soon as all arrangements can be made."

Geoffrey glanced around quickly to see if anyone else was paying attention to this conversation, and was relieved to see the other men were finishing and heading toward the stables. "You do not mean to say…" He looked at the pair, not knowing how to ask about what he had begun to suspect.

Dunfred and Cortlyn exchanged looks, seemed to agree on something, and Cortlyn continued. "Leonore helps the people in the village in more ways than I can tell you. She delivers babies, helps the sick and keeps us safe from those who would harm us. We are more than happy to do what we can in return."

Dunfred took over the conversation. "Sometimes, Leonore needs a man to…to help her regain her strength. Not often, but sometimes. It is a great honor."

"And you do not mind?" Geoffrey's incredulous question was directed at Cortlyn.

"Oh, no!" Again, Cortlyn blushed. "It is well known that a man who has been…who has helped Leonore in that way…"

41

She stopped, looking at Dunfred for help. He took her hand and smiled warmly at her.

"Leonore has taught me to appreciate the pleasures of being with a woman, and how lucky I am to have Cortlyn. I cannot wait to be her husband."

"In our village, a girl who marries one of Leonore's favorites is envied." Cortlyn had recovered her power of speech. "They know they will have the most loving and faithful of husbands."

Geoffrey observed the tender look that passed between the pair with astonishment. These two were actually *grateful* to Leonore for having made Dunfred her lover. Further, Geoffrey realized their confession meant they knew *he* had been with Leonore, and considered that he and Dunfred now had something in common. Which, he supposed, they did.

At that moment, Leonore had come back from the kitchen carrying a small bundle, and Wilfred had come in with the news the horses were ready to go. Geoffrey had no opportunity to speak to Leonore privately, as he was obliged to gather his gear from her bedroom. By the time he returned, she was already mounted on her horse, as was the rest of the party.

Now, as the morning gave way to midday, he had still had no opportunity to speak with her without being overheard. She was behaving as if nothing special had taken place between them.

Which is exactly how you intended to ask her to behave, he reminded himself sourly. *She obviously had the good sense to figure it out on her own.* Or did she? Perhaps as far as she was concerned, what had passed the night before was nothing out of the ordinary, and not worth mentioning. He was unaware he was scowling until he heard the soft sound of hooves approaching to his right, and turned to find himself abreast with the very person who was causing his discontent.

"You look worried about something, Sir Geoffrey. Is anything amiss?" Leonore's cheery tone held no hint of sarcasm.

"No, nothing." Geoffrey quickly relaxed his furrowed brow. "I just wanted to speak to you about...about what we may expect to find when we arrive at the castle."

"All right." Leonore settled her horse into a path and pace that matched Geoffrey's. The forest trail had widened to something more akin to a road, and they urged their horses forward to put some space between themselves and the others.

"King Liam is entertaining his allies at present. He has been holding court for more than two weeks as he discusses his plans to swear fealty to the High King. Do you understand what that will mean?"

"Yes," said Leonore, "and I am heartily pleased to hear it. But I would guess not all of his allies share my view on the subject."

"Aye, and you would be right." Geoffrey would have stood by any decision King Liam made, but he was in complete accordance with the king's admiration and respect for the young High King of Britain. He was attempting to unite all the small kingdoms and other holdings in an effort to restore the peace that had evaded the isles since the departure of the Romans more than a century before. King Liam was the most powerful leader in this part of the isles, and had forged alliances, mostly genial, with the surrounding kings, dukes and self-styled rulers. His cooperation was crucial to the High King's plans, but he would have a job ahead of him convincing some of his more troublesome allies to go along with him. It was one of these, no doubt, who had engineered Prince Wesley's disappearance.

"And I suppose you can identify the most likely suspects." Leonore's question told Geoffrey she was easily following his line of thinking.

"Yes, but it is not those who openly oppose him that trouble me. If it turns out to be someone like Lorimar, who has always been a problem, or King Balan, then no one will be overtroubled if Liam has to take action." Geoffrey waited for Leonore's nod and then continued. "What I really fear is that someone who pretends to be the king's friend — someone who always agrees with him publicly — is making their own plans."

"Is there someone in particular you distrust? You seem like a man with good instincts."

Geoffrey smiled. "Do your own instincts tell you that?"

"They do."

Geoffrey shook his head. "Well, I am afraid mine have failed me in this instance. I have run this problem around and around in my mind until I see traitorous thoughts in everyone's eyes. Many of the king's supporters are doubtless completely sincere and loyal to their oaths. Others..." He shrugged.

"Well, that is why you have *me*." Leonore's musical laugh was at odds with the seriousness of the conversation. "I have never met any of these men before, and know little of their history with King Liam. I should be able to read them without prejudice."

Geoffrey kept his counsel on the subject of Leonore's ability to "read" the men who currently sat at Liam's court. By the light of day, the magic that had seemed quite reasonable when sitting in Leonore's beautiful bathing pool — or lying in her bed — seemed a distant and foolish notion. Another thought struck Geoffrey.

"I wonder," he said, voicing his thought aloud, "what Chellasandre and Wallix will think of you."

"Who are they?"

"King Liam's mystics." Geoffrey gave a short, scornful laugh. "I have never seen either of them produce anything but unpleasant-smelling smoke and predictions so general, no one could say they held no truth. But for some reason I do not understand, the king keeps them around. They are not going to be happy to find out he has so little faith in their abilities that he has sent for reinforcements." The thought quite cheered Geoffrey, who had reason to dislike the mystics. Whatever his opinion of Leonore — and he was not at all sure he knew what that was — he had a notion she would be more than a match for the two self-important charlatans.

"I look forward to meeting them," said Leonore sweetly, and Geoffrey grinned at her too-dulcet tones.

"Not as much as I look forward to it, I'll warrant." With that, he slowed the horse's pace and allowed the others to catch up. Soon Leonore had fallen back, and he could hear her laughing merrily as Wilfred serenaded her with an off-key rendition of a bawdy soldier's song. Geoffrey realized he had quite forgotten he was annoyed with her.

* * * * *

"And *that* is when young Geoffrey fell off the horse!" Wilfred finished his tale with a hearty laugh, followed by guffaws by the men and a wry smile from the tale's subject.

"That's not exactly the way I remember it," said Geoffrey, "but I do remember falling off the horse. My arse was sore for a week."

"That was more probably due to the walloping your father gave you for stealing the horse in the first place." Wilfred stood and yawned enormously. "Well, lads, you wanted me to show you how to make a shelter from a willow tree. I saw a big one just the other side of that hill. Pick up your packs and we will sleep there this night."

"We need no shelter tonight," argued Horace. "It is warm for spring. We could have done without the fire, had we not shot the rabbits." He patted his bow, justifiably proud of his marksmanship.

"If you wait until you need it, it will be too late for the lesson," growled the old knight, and the two younger men followed him reluctantly away from the fire. Geoffrey and Leonore said their goodnights, and watched them go.

"I think," said Geoffrey, "that Wilfred has conspired to leave us alone."

Leonore was surprised to feel a hot blush rise to her cheeks. "Do you think he heard us last night?" She was not embarrassed about lovemaking—not usually, anyway. But last night she had been...well, she had given no thought to the sounds she made.

"I think he is a canny man and knows when his presence is not required." Geoffrey went through the pack he had removed from his horse and, finding a wineskin, turned back to Leonore. He took a sip then passed it to her. "Cortlyn filled this for me before we left. I did not have enough to share with the full company, but it is unlikely to improve with age once in the skin."

"I should have thought to bring a cask for the king. The villagers send him a tribute, of course, but usually not the wine." Leonore took a sip of the wine, her eyes on Geoffrey's. He had been annoyed with her earlier, she was quite sure. He had passed it off as concern about what awaited them at King Liam's castle, but she felt it was more than that.

Watching as he settled his back against a boulder, Leonore wondered what had set off Geoffrey's annoyance. He had been happy to share her bed, and her body tingled with both the memory of what they had done and what they might yet do. But something had changed—what was it?

Leonore replayed the day in her mind. She had arisen early, despite a night that had included little sleep. She smiled, remembering how incongruous it had been to see such a masculine man looking so angelic in sleep. Then she had given instructions to Cortlyn, made her final traveling arrangements and gathered some herbs from her garden. When she had next seen Geoffrey, he had been sitting at the table with Cortlyn and...

Dunfred! Leonore, distracted with her preparations, had noticed but given no mind to the earnest expressions on the faces of the three people conversing at the table. Cortlyn and Dunfred must have told Geoffrey about their arrangement with her. That would explain his odd behavior on the trail this morning.

Again, Leonore felt the heat rise to her face, albeit for a different reason. She searched her mind for a label for the unfamiliar emotion and found it. *Embarrassment!* Instantly, Leonore was cross with herself. *Why should I care what he thinks of the way I manage my magic? I have made no secret of the nature of my power.*

"What are you thinking about, Leonore?" Geoffrey's voice caused her to start, which he obviously noticed, as his expression changed to a grin.

Leonore, her composure regained, let her face match his. "Why do you ask, Sir Knight? A woman may choose not to answer such a question." She was pleased to note her teasing tone revealed nothing of the discomfort she was feeling.

"Your brow was knotted as if trying to solve a particularly bothersome riddle. I could not imagine what was making such a beautiful face look so annoyed on such a beautiful night. And with such fine company."

Leonore laughed in genuine relief. "You are right, Geoffrey. The night—and the company—are too fine to waste on puzzling thoughts. I would rather concentrate on other things."

"Other things?" Geoffrey's raised his eyebrows and wiggled them comically. "Surely, after all day on a horse, you are exhausted and wish to go to sleep as soon as may be."

"Oh, I am accustomed to riding horseback. I may not be a knight, but I have traveled many miles in a saddle, and a pleasant ride like we had today does little more than make me want to stretch my limbs a bit after dismounting."

"Indeed." Geoffrey put down the wineskin and reached across Leonore's legs to place a hand on the outside of each thigh. "When my horse is stiff after a hard day's ride, the stable boy massages the muscles in his haunches. Perhaps such a treatment would benefit you as well."

"Are you comparing me to your horse, Geoffrey?" Leonore pretended insult, but the pressure of his hands on her legs was causing a stirring that made the control of her voice increasingly difficult.

"My horse? Well, you are both beautiful animals of obviously fine breeding. You both like to be ridden…"

At this, Leonore attempted to give him a playful slap, but Geoffrey caught her hand and placed it on the swelling beneath his braies with barely a pause in his words.

"…and you both like to choose who your riders will be!"

Before Leonore could think of an answer to this ribald comment, Geoffrey's mouth was on hers, tasting of wine and salt and maleness.

A vortex engulfed her. *Again?* Leonore struggled against the forces that seemed to strip her of all control whenever this man touched her. *Why is it different with you, Geoffrey?* She could no more have voiced the words at this moment than she could have flown.

She felt Geoffrey shudder, and realized the hand that had been gripping his shaft through the trousers had involuntarily tightened until she was squeezing rather than caressing. As one of Geoffrey's hands found its way under her kirtle and began to move up her bare thigh, she used both hands to free his swelling member from the prison of the braies. It throbbed in her hands, and she reached one hand down to caress the sack that hung below its silky hardness.

"Aaaah." Geoffrey purred like a big cat, and eased Leonore onto her back so that he could lift the skirts of her kirtle above her waist. He shifted his own weight to the side, so she did not have to relinquish her grip even as he pulled up one of her knees, exposing the opening of her womanhood to the night air.

Leonore shuddered as the cooling breeze struck the soft, wet folds of skin that were still slightly swollen from Geoffrey's ministrations the night before. She realized Geoffrey's hands had stopped moving, and opened her eyes to find him leaning his weight against one arm, staring at her hungrily. One of her hands still encircled his cock, and his eyes narrowed slightly as she reached the top of each stroke, but he never looked away.

"What do you see?" she managed to say without gasping.

"Perfection," he replied. He reached out a hand to stroke the damp curls between her legs, letting one finger linger where the soft lips surrounding her slitted opening met. He let the finger pull lightly, sending arrows of heat through her limbs and awakening a deep pulsing in the depths of her body.

Leonore threw her head back and groaned. *I should be doing this to him*, she thought vaguely. *He should be the one feeling he cannot wait another moment for...*

Before Leonore could form another coherent thought, Geoffrey abruptly shifted his weight and slid the head of his shaft into her. She felt wetness erupt from deep within her like a fountain, making him slide into her as easily as if she was filled with warm butter.

I will be lost in this ecstasy. I will never find my way back. The world disappeared, leaving nothing but sensation. As Geoffrey slid his hot, slick cock into her again and again, it seemed like each stroke brought him deeper. She could feel him against every inch of her inner places, pressing against her very womb. Her hands grasped his buttocks roughly, trying to pull him yet deeper into her body. She was vaguely aware of the wet sounds of their coming together and the moans that seemed to be made by other voices but were their own.

"Spill your seed into me, Geoffrey!" she managed to pant, aware of the ragged sound of her voice but beyond caring. With a cry, Geoffrey obeyed her command, and she felt the hot explosion of liquid that seemed as if would fill her until she burst.

Chapter Five

❧

King Liam's castle was not the first Leonore had seen, nor the largest, although she had no intention of sharing this particular bit of information with Geoffrey. It was, however, one of the most pleasant. The palisade that surrounded the lower part of the hill was low, and looked sturdy rather than forbidding. All gates stood open, and although the villagers made way for the party of knights, their mien was respectful rather than fearful. She was pleased when Geoffrey greeted some of the villagers by name, reinforcing her assessment of his character.

From around the corner of an outbuilding, with a great deal of deep and resonant barking, came a large pack of the most enormous dogs Leonore had ever seen. They barreled toward the riders and soon surrounded the horses, yapping and seeming to seek the attention of the knights. Leonore reined in her horse, concerned the enormous animals would startle him.

"Do not worry Leonore, they are friendly." Wilfred bent over in his saddle to stroke the head of one of the shaggy creatures. "They belong to the king, and have the run of the place when he does not hunt with them."

"I am pleased to hear they are friendly. They are almost as big as the horses!" Leonore replied, but she could see Wilfred spoke the truth about the creatures' friendliness.

The party rode under the open portcullis, and Leonore felt the tingle of anticipation as she sensed curious eyes upon her. She had ceased her banter with the knights as soon as they had reached the borders of the village in order to open her mind and read the reactions of the local people. Thus far, she felt no apprehension at the knights' appearance, and little more than passing interest in her own person. From everyone other than Geoffrey, of course. His emotions had ranged from confusion to annoyance.

I really must speak with him alone at the first opportunity. Leonore knew Geoffrey did not know what to make of her and, to a certain extent, she found his bewilderment delicious. He had been a delightful surprise, both in bed and out, and she intended to enjoy both his company and his caresses as often and for as long as possible. Right now, however, her duty was to the king. *I will attend to Geoffrey later. It is not important what he thinks about me right now.*

Leonore was surprised to find she was attempting to convince herself. She *did* care what this exceptional man thought about her. The realization was so unanticipated that for a moment she forgot to pay attention to the thought impressions she had been allowing to drift over her consciousness. Suddenly, a crashing wave of hostility hit her with an icy force that caused her to catch her breath and stiffen with shock. Her horse, sensitive to her every movement, snorted and pulled up.

"What is it?" asked Geoffrey, who had glanced back in time to see the horse's hesitation.

"Someone is watching us. Someone who *hates* one of us—probably you, since it is too strong to be anything but personal." Regaining her composure, Leonore put a smile on her face and turned toward Geoffrey as if she was sharing a pleasant story. "Do not look around so sharply, Geoffrey, or they will perceive your suspicions."

Geoffrey nodded curtly and put a forced smile on his face. Leonore supposed it would pass from a distance, if one did not take his rigid posture into account. "Can you tell who it is?"

"Not precisely—I do not know anyone here. But it feels distinctly feminine. Are any of the king's allies women?"

"No, although some have their wives or daughters with them. Who...?" Geoffrey trailed off, and Leonore saw his expression change as he caught sight of something or someone in their path.

"You can relax, Leonore. It is indeed someone who hates me, but it has nothing to do with Wesley's disappearance." A sardonic smile, this time quite real, settled over his handsome features.

Leonore looked around to see who he referred to, and saw two figures standing at the foot of a stone stairs that led into what had to be the main court. At first glance, the two could have been brother and sister, but Leonore quickly realized the resemblance was only an illusion caused by their attire, similar coloring and intense stares.

Both were dressed very grandly, wearing heavy robes detailed in elaborate patterns with metallic threads that glittered in the sun. Much too heavy, Leonore thought dryly, for the warm spring day. The woman's complicated headdress looked more fitting for a grand ceremony than a casual greeting, if that was what this was.

As the mounted group approached, the tall man, his skin very white against his glittering black robe and hair, slowly raised his hands until they were parallel to his face in what appeared to be a practiced gesture. He looked like a pagan high priest about to bestow a blessing — or a curse.

"Sir Geoffrey." The voice that rang out in the barbican had an unnatural timbre that matched the pose of its originator. "We are most relieved to see you back safe and well."

"And why should I be otherwise?" said Geoffrey in normal tones. "I was on but a small journey, and expected no especial danger."

"So we were informed," continued the pale man, still in his theatrical tone. "But in these uncertain times, when you left with an escort of three of our most venerated knights," at this description, a snort Leonore recognized as Wilfred's was audible, "we could not but wonder if perhaps your errand was more dangerous than His Majesty implied."

Geoffrey remained unperturbed, at least on the surface. "I thought you had the ear of the king in all matters, Wallix? You have certainly said as much to anyone who would listen. Is there some reason King Liam would keep the reason for my journey from you?" Leonore heard a hissed intake of breath as Geoffrey's barb hit home. Wallix stiffened visibly and seemed temporarily at a loss for words. He seemed to realize his hands were still raised in the ceremonial pose, and lowered them slowly.

"King Liam holds our counsel in the highest regard, no thanks to you." The small woman's voice was high pitched but not displeasing, even with the light touch of venom it contained. Leonore observed her closely for the first time. "If you think we do not know you take every opportunity to undermine us, *Sir* Geoffrey, then you are sadly mistaken." Geoffrey's title was fairly spit out. Even had she not already felt it, Leonore would have known this woman despised Geoffrey.

"I have made no secret of it," was Geoffrey's amiable rejoinder. "You waste the king's time with your dire predictions and so-called magic. I have urged him to rid himself of your poisonous presence for years, although for some reason I cannot fathom, he has thus far resisted my advice. Not that I intend to stop trying."

"I have a dire prediction for *you*, you arrogant bastard!" Chellasandre's voice was no longer pleasant. "You will be sorry you doubted my magic when it comes down upon your conceited head!"

"Chellasandre." Wallix's melodious voice interrupted, and a pale hand was placed upon Chellasandre's arm, which she had raised as if to cast a curse. "Do not allow this ignorant unbeliever to incite you."

Leonore was impressed. Wallix had the ability to speak in a tone that was, on the surface, conversational, but rang to every corner of the courtyard so everyone heard him clearly. She wondered what other powers he had. Nothing she could discern, but she would have to touch him to be sure. Certainly he despised Geoffrey, but not with the visceral intensity that flowed from Chellasandre.

She felt that hatred waver and break as a new emotion leapt to replace it—suspicion. "Who are *you?*" Chellasandre's narrowed eyes focused on Leonore for the first time. "Do you have something to do with Geoffrey's errand for the king?"

"Why do you ask?" Leonore responded to the question in a light tone, and felt the suspicion sharpen into hostility. To her astonishment, she realized Chellasandre was trying to probe *her* mind, although not very effectively. Still, she could feel a slight brush of power. *Not entirely without magic after all.* Leonore instantly closed her mind to the feeble probing.

Chellasandre's head snapped back as if she had been slapped. Her eyes opened wide and darkened with anger. "You are a *witch!*" she hissed. "King Liam has sent for a *witch!*" She whirled to face Wallix. "Did you know of this? Has he so little faith in our abilities that he brought in an *outsider?* He has not even given us the chance to find — "

"Chellasandre!" thundered Wallix, cutting her off in mid-sentence. "You forget yourself!" His voice lowered, he continued, "We do not know who may be observing." Chellasandre was obviously stung by his reprimand, but held her tongue and turned hostile eyes on Leonore.

Wallix continued. "Perhaps, Geoffrey, you should bring your *guest* to the main hall, so we can discuss her reasons for being here."

"I indeed intend to escort her to the hall, but only because she is to wait upon King Liam. My orders are to bring her to him, not to you." Geoffrey signaled to a young man who had been watching the verbal sparring match with apparent enjoyment. Immediately, he came and took the reins of Geoffrey's horse, and the knight dismounted. "Take the lady's as well," he said, and the man nodded and would have helped

Leonore dismount, but she did so smoothly on her own and handed him the reins.

Ignoring Wallix and Chellasandre, Leonore and Geoffrey took a few moments to select some small items from their packs before the horses were led away by the man, who turned out to be Geoffrey's squire, Ronuld. Geoffrey chatted with him for a moment about the health of his wife and new son, whose recent arrival had excused Ronuld from the journey to fetch Leonore. Leonore suppressed a giggle when she saw from the corner of her eye that the two mystics, frustrated at the delay, had stalked up the stairs and departed, enfolding the remains of their tattered dignity around them.

"It was kind of you to let your squire stay at home with his wife and child," she told Geoffrey once Ronuld had departed and he had dismissed the rest of the men. "Not many knights would do the same."

"It is his first child, and the birth was very difficult. With his wife still recovering, he would have been too distracted to be of any use." Geoffrey shrugged off the compliment, but Leonore knew few men of noble birth would have considered the feelings of a mere squire. It was just another example of the quality of this man.

"Geoffrey, before I meet with the king, I want to speak with you about our nights together."

"I will not mention them to King Liam, if that is what you fear." Geoffrey's tone was casual, but his quick response made Leonore think the topic was much on his mind.

"Of course you will not mention it. You are far too fine a man to do so." She smiled prettily, and was rewarded with a look of mild embarrassment. "I just wanted you to know our time together thus far has been very special to me, and I yearn to be with you again — in that way — as soon as may be. But this business for the king may take all of my attention for a while, and it may seem as if I am ignoring you." Seldom at a loss for words, Leonore struggled a little to find the right way to phrase what she must say.

"Please know nothing would make me happier than to find a private bed and…well, you know what I would like to do then!" Geoffrey actually blushed, and she went on.

"But if I have to do any serious magic, I cannot even allow the thoughts to enter my mind. I may become very focused and seem abrupt. If that happens, it will have nothing to do with you."

Obviously discomfited by this speech, Geoffrey nodded and hesitated, as if he too were having trouble finding the right words. "It has been special to me as well, Leonore," he finally said. "But I did not travel to Caernham to find a lover — although that *was* a wonderful surprise. I went to find someone my king thought could help him. I hope you are that person."

"As do I," replied Leonore, and she turned in the direction of the stairs. "As we are in complete accord, shall we go see the king?" she asked. Geoffrey proffered an arm and she took it without hesitation. As they ascended the short flight of steps, he spoke again.

"You know at this very moment Chellasandre and Wallix are waiting in the hall, plotting how they can discredit you before the king."

"I look forward to it." Leonore held her head a little higher and laughed, and Geoffrey joined her. As they walked through the arch that was the entrance to the main court, their laughter echoed against the stone walls.

* * * * *

The main hall of King Liam's castle was large and had a high ceiling, and the tables that were used for court feasts were in place, though bare. *So the king's allies are still in residence,* thought Leonore. *I wonder where they are.* At the front of the hall, Chellasandre and Wallix had seated themselves at the king's table as if they were ready to hold their own court. Leonore thought this tactic too obvious to be effective, and

Geoffrey apparently agreed with her, as he ignored the head table entirely and walked with her to the head of one of the lower tables, as he pointed out the features of the hall.

"The tapestry is amazing." Leonore stepped closer to the wall to view it more closely. "It is Moorish, is it not? How on earth did Kind Liam come by such a thing?"

"And just how would you know it is Moorish?" Wallix's interrupting voice was less theatrical without an audience, but still impressive. "Are you so well traveled?"

"Perhaps a bit more than the average person," replied Leonore without looking at the speaker. "But a man may never see a vineyard and yet recognize good wine when he tastes it." Having answered and avoided the question at the same time, she turned back to Geoffrey, continuing to ignore Wallix. "I'll be fine here while you go and tell the king of my arrival."

Geoffrey looked at her sharply, obviously reluctant to leave her alone with the scheming mystics. With her head still turned away from Wallix and Chellasandre, she solemnly lowered one eyelid and winked. Geoffrey's mouth quirked, but he did not laugh.

"As you wish, Leonore. I will not be long." He strode off toward an archway behind the dais, and Leonore continued her study of the tapestry. *It really is Moorish. The last time I saw one so fine was in the home of that emir in Cordoba...what was his name?* Leonore's reverie was interrupted by the sound of a chair being pushed back. Apparently, either Wallix or Chellasandre had gotten tired of waiting for her to stand before the dais like a subject, and had decided to come to her. She pretended to be lost in thought as she listened to the sound of feet cross the floor. A woman's footfall, she decided.

"You and Sir Geoffrey seem to get along very well," purred Chellasandre as she stood next to Leonore as if she, too, were examining the tapestry for the first time. "Do not grow too accustomed to it. He does not believe in magic, you know, and will soon show his true character."

Ah, that explains it. Leonore turned to study the smaller woman as closely as she had been scrutinizing the drapery. *There was something between her and Geoffrey. Something that had not ended in a way she liked.*

Chellasandre, who had no doubt stepped down from the dais with the intention of being the observer rather than the observed, chafed visibly under Leonore's examination. "Why do you not answer me?"

Leonore raised her eyebrows, all innocence. "I am sorry. I did not realize you were expecting an answer. Was there a question?"

Chellasandre paused, apparently realizing she had not actually asked Leonore anything. Quickly, she asked, "Why has the king sent for you? What does he think you can do that we cannot?"

"I would not presume to know King Liam's mind," Leonore shrugged. "I do not even know how he learned of my reputation."

"Your reputation? I have never heard of you." Chellasandre's tone seemed intended to start an argument, but Leonore refused to rise to the bait.

"Few have," she replied, "and yet it seems the king is among them. I shall have to wait and hear what he has to say."

"How did Geoffrey explain it?" Chellasandre was beginning to sound genuinely curious. Leonore shrugged again.

"I did not ask. We were rather too...*occupied* to discuss details." Leonore could not resist the gentle emphasis she placed on the word, and was gratified when a subtle narrowing of Chellasandre's eyes indicated she had not missed the implication. "In any case, I am here now, and King Liam will no doubt make his wishes clear when he sees me."

"*If* he sees you." Leonore was startled to learn that Wallix had come up on her opposite side while her attention was turned to Chellasandre. *I must give him credit for stealth,* she thought ruefully. Knowing it was too late to hide her surprise, as her shoulders stiffened at his words she smiled slightly and gave a tiny dip of her head, as if conceding a point to him. *Which is*, she reflected, *exactly what I am doing.*

"He sent four knights to bring me here," said Leonore. "I would assume he has a reason to speak with me."

"I am sure he believed so when he sent for you," replied Wallix, "but King Liam counts upon Chellasandre and myself to divine whether those who would come before him bear him any ill will. We have yet to determine whether you are his friend or his enemy."

"Since His Majesty puts so much faith in you," said Leonore, "it must have come as quite a shock when someone — presumably someone whose presence you approved — abducted his son right out of the castle."

This was, as Leonore had expected, a direct hit. Wallix's equanimity vanished, and his eyes seemed to bulge from his skull as his voice lost all melody. "We do not know he was abducted. He may have been made to vanish through sorcery!"

Leonore laughed her tinkling laugh, which seemed to infuriate Wallix even more. "I feel sure I know a great deal more about sorcery, as you call it, than you will ever know, Wallix. And even I do not believe magic can make a man disappear."

"I have seen it done," said Chellasandre, coming to the defense of Wallix, who appeared to be too angry to speak.

"As have I," said Leonore. "Many times. Also pigs, doves and, once, a small wagon. But these were mere tricks performed by illusionists — talented and skillful men, I must admit. They know how to distract the gullible mind and trick the untutored eye. But they do nothing truly magical."

"How *dare* you compare yourself to me, woman!" A thunderous voice announced that Wallix had regained his powers of speech. "You know not whom you challenge!"

Wallix stood very straight and raised his hands to point toward Leonore. He filled his lungs with air and opened his eyes very wide, lowering his chin so a considerable amount of white showed below the dark pupils. He seemed to get taller, and Leonore saw, to her amusement, that he was gradually rising to his toes.

Leonore felt a disturbance in the air, like a breeze that was trying to blow but could not get started. Then it was still, and Leonore realized what had happened. She felt a burst of laughter well up in her chest and was unable to contain her amusement.

Her laugh rang out, loud and raucous and filled with delight. "Oh, Wallix! Are you actually trying to summon a *glamour* to frighten me?" The sight of the pale man trying to inflate himself was too much for Leonore, and again her laugh trilled musically through the hall.

Wallix was unable to sustain both his unnatural pose and his rage simultaneously, and exhaled audibly as he sank back on his heels. Before he could regain his composure, Leonore saw a blur of motion as Chellasandre leapt in front of her, seething. "Wallix is a great magician, and you have no right to ridicule him!"

Leonore raised her eyebrows. "I did not start this confrontation, Chellasandre. I came here to help my king. You claim to wish to do the same. If that is true, then you should be happy for any help I can offer."

"I have yet to see any evidence you *can* help," countered Chellasandre. "Perhaps you have no abilities that will be of any use."

"Perhaps," replied Leonore. "But I think you already know differently. I do not know if Wallix here has any talent beyond the power of his voice and the ability to move swiftly and silently." Wallix started to splutter but Leonore cut him off. "*You*, however, have some real power. Not very strong, I think, but strong enough that you tried to perceive my mind and knew exactly when I stopped you. Am I wrong?"

Chellasandre managed to preen herself at Leonore's acknowledgement of her power and look disdainful at the same time. She was obviously searching for a really stinging retort when Wallix interrupted.

"Chellasandre is *my* apprentice," said Wallix, his mellifluous tones back in place. "Do not assume just because you have been unable to perceive my power, it does not exist. I have had more years to learn to shield it."

"I think not. I felt it quite clearly when your feeble attempt at a glamour sputtered." This man was really starting to annoy Leonore. Chellasandre was, at least, interesting.

"What would you know of building a glamour?" Wallix seemed fully in control of his composure. "It takes considerable effort, and I simply decided you were not worth the trouble."

This self-important fool has become exceedingly boring. Leonore had not intended to make any display of her power to these two charlatans, but had become tired of their tedious posturing and insults. *Maybe just a tiny display. Even Wallix has enough power to feel mine if it is placed directly in front of his nose.* She turned to face him and stepped back so she could see both Wallix's and Chellasandre's faces at the same time.

"Considerable effort, you say? Perhaps, Wallix, you are trying too hard. A glamour is really a very simple thing. Here, let me demonstrate." Leonore reached into the air around her and drew the power so quickly, neither Wallix nor Chellasandre had a chance to do more than take a single step back as their eyes opened wide and their jaws literally dropped. *Ah, well. Self-control was never my best trait.* She smiled inwardly in satisfaction as she pulled the first tendrils of the glamour around her.

Chapter Six

❧

"I am sure Leonore expected to be summoned to your antechamber," said Geoffrey to King Liam as they approached the arch leading to the steps behind the main hall's dais. "She will be surprised at you coming down to meet her."

"When you told me Wallix and Chellasandre were unhappy about her presence, I thought it would be better to meet with all of them at once. And I did not want to have the whole group brought before me—it would incite too much comment. Besides," King Liam's chuckle was a deep rumble in his chest, "it is not often I get to see my mystics discomfited, and I could not resist."

"Why you bother to keep those two vultures around is beyond me," said Geoffrey, and Liam raised his hand to forestall the oft-heard argument.

"As I have told you before, Geoffrey, they are the best I have found. I know well their powers are limited, but they do have magic."

Geoffrey held his counsel. He and the king were unlikely to ever agree on this topic, and it was a testament to their long friendship that Liam gave him the latitude to voice his opinion. Friends or no, there was no doubt who was the king and who was the vassal, and Geoffrey knew he must choose his battles carefully.

"Well, I think you will find Leonore to be an interesting contrast. As short a time as I have known her, I would venture to say she would laugh at the notion of calling herself a 'mystic'. She found the term 'witch' amusing enough. But as for calling whatever it is she does magic…"

Geoffrey's words trailed off as he came to a dead halt at the top of the steps. His mind tried to register what his eyes were seeing, and failed. The king, finding his path blocked by his escort, spoke in an irritated tone.

"Geoffrey, why do you stand like a stone? I am half on the steps and half on the dais…" As King Liam brushed impatiently past the unmoving knight, he turned his face toward the sight that had temporarily paralyzed his friend. "By all the gods," he whispered. "Finally, what I have sought for all these years."

Gradually, Geoffrey perceived the sight that confronted them. Leonore was standing with her back to the Moorish tapestry, her attention on the two mystics who stood as if they were chained in place. Their eyes held terror, but they did not look away from Leonore.

Nor could Geoffrey. Despite the dim light of the hall, which was lighted only by torches and the waning rays of the sun through the upper window slits, she seemed to shine as if standing under the noonday sun. Light glinted off her coppery curls and the deep green of her eyes glowed as with an inner fire. She appeared to have grown in stature until she towered like a giantess over the two who stood before her. She seemed to float, although Geoffrey could see that her feet touched the floor. Though no wind moved through the hall, the torches flickered and Leonore's clothes billowed slightly around her as her tresses lifted lightly from her shoulders.

There was something more, however, something less tangible but much, much more powerful about her. He had thought her beautiful from the first time he had seen her, but her beauty had been that of a comely woman, sensual and earthy. Now it seemed somehow terrible, as if to gaze at her too long would blind a mere man. Like an angel—or a demon. Geoffrey felt himself shudder with the memory that he had held that very woman in his arms, tasted her, smelled her— even emptied his seed into her. How could he not have been burned, as if he had tried to embrace a fiery blaze?

He perceived the movement of the king as he stepped forward to the front of the dais and closer to Leonore's line of vision. "Lady..." started the king quietly, then louder, "Leonore."

Slowly, Leonore turned her head to face the two men, and Wallix and Chellasandre seemed to relax, although they still seemed rooted in place. For the briefest of seconds, Geoffrey felt a strange rush of power as her gaze swept over him. Then her face changed, and suddenly she was just a woman. A beautiful, noble woman, but mortal and real and no longer frightening. Wallix and Chellasandre slumped, and the older man would have fallen had his apprentice not grabbed his arm.

"Your Majesty." Leonore sank into a deep curtsey and lowered her head before the king.

"Please rise," said King Liam, sounding slightly dazed. As Leonore arose, she did not wait for his words, but spoke.

"I must apologize for using magic in your home without your leave. It was unforgivable, and I promise it will not happen again." Liam did not respond immediately, and she lifted her face to look at him.

"I will accept both your apology and your promise," said the king, sounding anything but angry. "I had intended to ask for a demonstration of your power, but I would have preferred to wait until we were alone." He smiled wryly. "I also had intended to ask Wallix and Chellasandre if they were able to perceive your power. I believe that is no longer necessary."

"Your Majesty, this...this woman..." Wallix stuttered, trying to find his dignity. He shook Chellasandre's supporting arm away in irritation. "This *witch* has assaulted your most trusted advisers under your very roof, and I demand she be held accountable!"

"Are you going to tell me the two of you did nothing to provoke her, Wallix?" King Liam's tone held no hint of sarcasm, and Wallix was in any case too angry to heed any subtle warning.

"Only our duty, Your Majesty. We needed to make sure she did not wish you harm and she would not cooperate."

"I see." Geoffrey watched intently as Liam turned to Leonore, who seemed unperturbed by the accusation and the scrutiny. "What have you to say, Leonore?"

"What he says may well be true, Your Majesty," said Leonore, to Geoffrey's astonishment. "I felt their intentions were more personally hostile, but I may have drawn the wrong conclusion." She looked sincerely contrite, and Geoffrey felt his own indignation begin to rise as she continued. "I am afraid I may have let my pride get the better of me. It was, as I said, unforgivable."

"Oh, come, Leonore, you know perfectly well you did not misinterpret their intentions!" Geoffrey, no longer able to witness Leonore apologizing for defending herself, felt the words burst from his mouth unbidden. "We had no more than passed the gate when you felt their hatred. You told me as much."

Both the interrupted Leonore and King Liam had turned toward Geoffrey in surprise, and Leonore was the first to find her voice. "Why, Geoffrey! I thought you did not believe in my magic."

"I did not," said Geoffrey. "And I am still not sure what I believe. But Your Majesty," Geoffrey said as he turned his appeal to the king, "anyone could have seen their ill will — it certainly did not require magic. And when they realized you had sent for someone to do what they could not — "

"You do not know we could not find Wesley on our own!" Chellasandre's childlike voice was shrill with anger. "We still have many spells to try, and — "

"Peace!" King Liam's deep voice rose to an alarming volume. He lowered it again and said, "I have had enough trouble explaining Wesley's absence at court without you announcing it in the main hall." When Chellasandre wilted under his angry stare, he slowly turned to survey the hall, still thankfully empty. He continued.

"You may continue with your spells, as long as no one divines what you are about. I have not stopped you. But I wish to see what Leonore can learn about my son's whereabouts, and the sooner the better. As long as you can keep your silence, you can come along. But one more word out of either one of you, and I will send you to your quarters. Understood?"

Chellasandre nodded sullenly and, after one last venomous look at Leonore, Wallix inclined his head in agreement. Sighing, King Liam turned back to Leonore.

"Now, I had intended to greet you more formally, and to welcome you to my home. You were recommended to me most highly, but we will discuss that later. The most important business now is to find my son. If you have no objections, we will begin immediately."

"Of course." Leonore spoke briskly. "If I could be taken to the place where he was last known to be, I will do what I can."

"Excellent. Sir Geoffrey, if you would lead us." The king held out his arm and Geoffrey, after a curt nod, stepped off the dais and went through a side door. He turned back to see the king indicating for Leonore to precede him, before following her through the arch into the dim passage that led to the winding stairs of the north bastion. He did not look back to see if Chellasandre and Wallix followed, but he doubted they would let Leonore out of their sight until they had no other choice.

Prince Wesley had chosen a room far from the more luxurious quarters of the main tower, which had surprised Geoffrey at the time. While he liked the young man who would someday sit on the throne, he had always thought of Wesley as a bit spoiled. The castle was filled with people eager to indulge every whim of the king's only offspring, and the boy had never been above taking advantage of this. Now in his early manhood, Wesley was still more than a little impetuous.

I suppose he chose this room for its privacy. I am sure there are plenty of girls who think to catch a future king's eye.

When he reached the door to the high room, Geoffrey turned to see that Chellasandre and Wallix had indeed followed. "Bring a torch, both of you," he commanded, and although their eyes flashed in a way that told him they resented taking orders from him, the king's warning was still too fresh for them to argue. They each removed a flaming torch from its sconce as they continued up the stairs. Geoffrey took the last one from the top of the stairs and entered the room.

It proved to be more luxurious than the last time Geoffrey had seen it. He supposed Wesley had found no reason why isolation should mean lack of comfort, and had cajoled or ordered servants to bring every luxury that could be carried up the narrow flight. Weavings hung from the walls, designed to block the chill that emanated from the thick stones. Rugs and furs covered the floor, and a bed that had to have been brought up in pieces dominated the center of the room. Geoffrey could not help but grin—Wesley had obviously tried to rival his father's famous sleeping chamber, in much smaller quarters and with less to work with. Nevertheless, it was impressive.

The bedclothes were rumpled but the room was otherwise tidy. "Has anyone disturbed the room since Wesley's disappearance?" asked Leonore.

"You will have to ask Wallix and Chellasandre," said King Liam. "Once I satisfied myself he was not here, and there was nothing to indicate a struggle, I kept all others out except for them."

"We disturbed nothing," said Wallix quickly. "We performed a spell there," he indicated a spot in the center of the rug that sat before the bed, "but when we received no certain...when we could not tell..." Wallix struggled to explain what had happened without using, Geoffrey was sure, the word "fail".

Chellasandre finished for him. "When our ritual did not result in divining the truth, we knew better than to move anything, so we could try again later. Everything is as we found it."

"Are these ashes from the ritual?" Leonore indicated a dark spot on the carpet, not in an accusatory fashion.

"No," said Chellasandre. "The...the spell did not require fire."

"It could have come from the brazier," suggested Wallix, indicating the small metal grate that sat on a bare patch of stone under the narrow window.

Leonore picked up some of the ash, rubbed it between her fingers and sniffed it carefully. She crinkled her nose, as if scenting something acrid. "No, this is not from firewood or charcoal. I do not recognize it but it reminds me of something familiar." She sniffed it again.

"Does it have anything to do with Wesley's disappearance?" asked the king, as Leonore held her fingers out so he and Geoffrey could also sniff the fragrant ash. Geoffrey could not identify the scent. Wallix and Chellasandre made no move to join them.

"I do not know. It may." Leonore went to the bed and ran her fingertips gently across the rumpled tangle of furs and linens that covered it. She closed her eyes and lifted the bedclothes up toward her face, where she held them against first one cheek and then the other. She held very still, and Geoffrey heard Wallix sigh with impatience, although he spoke no word.

Leonore stood without moving for what seemed like an interminable time, although it was in reality probably only a minute or two. Geoffrey could see the rise and fall of her breasts as she breathed deeply, and realized he had been holding his own breath. He managed to exhale without making too loud a sound. Again, it seemed as if a light shone upon Leonore, although it was not remotely as intense as what he had seen in the great hall. He realized his ears were ringing, and the room seemed to hold a faint pressure. He shook his head slightly, and saw from Liam's raised eyebrow that the king felt it as well.

When the tension grew almost unbearable, Geoffrey heard another impatient sigh behind him, and heard Chellasandre whisper to Wallix, "What is she doing?" Geoffrey started to turn to reprimand her, but Leonore stirred and opened her eyes. They seemed unfocused, and she spoke to no one and to everyone.

"He is in his bed. He cannot see their faces. Hands cover his nose and mouth...he cannot breathe. It feels as if his lungs will burst." She spoke in a monotone, as if in a trance.

"Something is in front of his face. It is on fire and it is smoking. He tries to turn his head away but someone holds it in place. At last, the hand over his mouth is released...he must breathe, he cannot prevent himself. The smoke burns his throat. He will cough it out, but...but again, a hand covers his mouth. Again, the burning as his lungs beg for air." Leonore breathed deeply as if trying to do what Wesley could not.

"Dizzy now...again, the hand moves and the smoking bundle is under his nose. Again, he can only pull the smoke deep into his lungs. The room grows dark..." Leonore's unfocused gaze wavered and suddenly her green eyes grew sharp. She blinked several times.

"I am sorry, King Liam. Wesley did not know who took him, at least not while he was still in this room. I was able to see what he saw, but it was only shadows and burning leaves held in a gloved hand." Again, she crouched and scraped up more of the ashes from the rug. "I know where I recognize the scent from now. It has been many years. The Spanish got it from the invaders, and I suppose it will grow in the southernmost reaches of their country. I have never seen it this far north."

Geoffrey was about to ask her if she had actually traveled to the land of the Spaniards, when Wallix interrupted. "Your

Majesty, she is attempting to deceive you. She is only saying aloud what we already guessed — Wesley was taken from sleep by unknown persons. It is convenient that she claims he never saw their faces, and there is no way to learn their identities."

Geoffrey was about to remind Wallix of the king's order that he remain silent when Leonore replied. "I did not say their identities could not be learned, only that Wesley did not know who took him. I had hoped to find out more without having to resort to stronger measures." She turned to Chellasandre and Wallix. "What spell did you try?"

Wallix looked a little taken aback at being consulted. To Geoffrey, Leonore's question had seemed genuine. Wallix apparently came to the same conclusion, as he answered her with slightly less arrogance than usual. "We cast a power circle, which is standard in...these sorts of spells."

"What did you use to seal the circle?" asked Leonore, surprising Geoffrey. Wallix hesitated, but Chellasandre answered.

"My hair," she said, then seemed to change her mind about what she was going to say next. "We cut some of my hair. We took it with us when we were done."

Leonore regarded her solemnly, and nodded. "Not a bad idea," she said slowly. "It might have worked, had the connection been one of blood."

Geoffrey had no idea what Leonore was speaking of, but Wallix and Chellasandre exchanged nervous looks and kept silent for once.

King Liam spoke impatiently. "Are you saying you have a method of learning more?"

"Yes," said Leonore, turning to him. "It is a fairly simple ritual, but it will require your participation, I think. You are Wesley's closest relative, and shared blood gives us the best chance."

"What must I do?" said King Liam, and Geoffrey felt alarm rise at the intense look that passed between Leonore and the king.

"My lord!" he said. "You must not put yourself in danger. It could be exactly what Wesley's abductors have in mind."

"He will be in no danger," said Leonore, never taking her eyes from Liam's. "But it may seem very strange to the uninitiated." After a moment of silence in which she and the king seemed to come to some unspoken understanding, Leonore turned to Geoffrey. "And we must be completely alone. Here, where it happened. Where Wesley's presence is the strongest. We must not be disturbed or distracted, no matter what you hear."

"If you think I am going to let my king participate in some unknown *ritual*, and not stay to protect him, you have greatly overestimated your influence with me!" Geoffrey felt himself growing more agitated, and was about to press his point when he felt Liam's hand on his arm.

"Sir Geoffrey," said the king quietly, silencing him. Liam seldom used the formal appellation outside of official affairs of court, and doing so now sent a message Geoffrey could not ignore. "When Leonore and I have been left alone, I will need you to make sure no one mounts the stairs. You will see that no one disturbs us until the ritual is done and we call for you. Is that understood?" Liam's tone brooked no disagreement.

Geoffrey looked from his sovereign to his lover, and saw no wavering in the expressions of either. Defeated, he sighed. "Yes, Your Majesty. It shall be as you wish."

"Good. Then we shall begin as soon as may be."

Geoffrey turned to see that Wallix and Chellasandre both looked as outraged as he felt, and almost laughed when he realized he was in agreement with them for the first time in their long and unhappy acquaintance.

Virginia Reede

Chapter Seven

Before Leonore was ready to start the ritual, she sent an unhappy Geoffrey for the small bundle of herbs she had packed at her cottage, and an even less cooperative Chellasandre for charcoal and a kettle of clean water she could heat on the small brazier. After all the others were again sent away, a fascinated King Liam sat on the bed as she selected various leaves and added them to the water to brew a fragrant tea.

"I have been under the impression that anything brewed for the purpose of casting a spell had to smell and taste horrible," he joked as the air became infused with a pleasant, astringent scent.

"I believe many otherwise sensible practitioners of herb lore add a couple of benign ingredients precisely for that purpose." Leonore smiled at the king, whom she was beginning to like. "It makes it more mysterious."

"What I saw in the great hall was mysterious enough to convince me." King Liam looked thoughtful. "Leonore, all I care about right now is the safety of my son, and to find out who is trying to undermine my plans to ally with the High King. But I have a great many questions for you about...what you do. And who you are."

"I will be happy to answer them," replied Leonore. "But we must prepare ourselves for the ritual. I will explain it to you as well as I can before we begin, but much of it cannot be expressed in words. It must be experienced." The earnestness on Liam's face made her smile again. "You have a love of magic, do you not?"

"Yes. You probably know I was not born to be king. I was the third son, and far enough removed from the throne that I had more freedom than my older brothers. So I traveled." His eyes took on a faraway look. "I crossed to the land of the Franks, then the Spaniards, and even to Andalus. There I saw…amazing things. Not all this smoke and chanting Wallix feels is necessary. But *real* magic. I had always intended to go back and find a magician who would consent to be my teacher. But then first my eldest brother was killed in a hunting accident, and my travels were cut short. When my remaining brother sickened and died…" He sighed. "My priorities changed. I had to put those plans out of my mind."

"Few would consider becoming a king a compromise of their plans," said Leonore. "But I can give you one gift, Your Majesty. This night, you will not only witness real magic, but perform it yourself. You will always remember what it feels like, and recognize it again should it ever cross your path. Does that please you?"

"More than I can tell you."

"Then let us prepare. The tea is done and needs only to cool." Leonore knelt on the rug before the bed and motioned for Liam to do the same opposite her. Between them, she placed a small bowl containing a paste of herbs she had ground with a pestle as the tea brewed. She pulled a miniature dagger with a jeweled hilt from her girdle and set it next to the bowl. On the opposite side, the cooling tea waited to be poured into a cup from Wesley's bedside table.

Leonore rose and removed her girdle and her outer kirtle, leaving only her chemise. She resettled on the carpet, wearing only her thin shift, and began daubing the bluish paste on her forehead and shoulders. "You will need to remove your tunic. There should be as little as possible against your skin."

"Will we need to be entirely naked?" asked Liam, complying.

"Not yet." Leonore saw the king's eyebrows rise, but continued. "As soon as the body wards are finished, we will drink the tea and cast the circle. Wallix and Chellasandre used hair, but I intend to use a much more powerful medium."

"What is that?" Liam held still as Leonore began making marks similar to her own on his face and chest.

"Your blood." When the king stiffened slightly in response, she went on. "Only a few drops will be needed, but they are the most important ingredient in the ritual and absolutely necessary." She felt Liam relax, and continued.

"As soon as the circle is closed, we must begin the rite immediately." Finished with the paste, she set it aside and filled the cup with the tea as she went on with her explanation. "The power circle will be the outer ring which contains and concentrates our magic. I am going to cast it around the bed because that is the last place where we know with certainty Wesley was alive and conscious." Holding the cup in one hand and the dagger in the other, she rose from her knees and gestured for the king to do the same.

"We will make all of the circle except for the final seal, then you and I will kneel in the middle of the bed. We will lean across and use a few more drop of blood to seal the circle, then face one another and join hands. This will create a second circle from which the power will flow."

"We are the inner circle? Our bodies?"

"Yes," said Leonore, pleased at the king's understanding. "And our minds. It is through us that the power will rise. All you need to do is keep your mind open and pay attention to what you see, hear, taste, smell and feel. If we are successful, all of your senses will be engaged."

"Should my eyes be open or closed?"

Leonore shook her head. "It will not matter. The pictures will be cast from within and you will see them regardless of what is before you. Now, King Liam, are you ready?"

The king breathed deeply and nodded. Leonore handed the cup to him and he drank. She took it from him and placed it against her own lips and drank all that remained. "Now we cast the circle." Beginning at one side of the bed, she took his hand in her own and carefully made a cut across the index finger of his left hand. As the blood welled up, she led him on a slow circle, making an uneven line of drops across the rugs and flagstones as they made their way around the bed in a counterclockwise circle. She stopped him before the line could join its beginning and, turning his hand palm up so the blood would not drip on the bedclothes, led him up on the bed.

Kneeling to face him, Leonore held his hand so the still-dripping blood landed in the palm of her hand. Leaning over the side of the bed, she spoke aloud the words she had learned so many years before.

"*Occlue nunc orbis, o caelestis! Pateo foris…arcesso animus…influxium valiturus!*" At the final word, she turned Liam's hand so the final drops of blood fell to the ground and closed the circle.

Instantly, the room seemed to shimmer and shift. Leonore saw the king's eyes widen, and before he could react in shock, she grasped both of his hands and pressed her bloodied palms against his. She held her arms wide and away from her body and threw her head back to face the ceiling, and felt the moment when the king understood and did the same. The inner circle abruptly completed, and the flow of power sprang to life, like a ball of glowing fire that warmed but did not burn, contained in the circle of their bodies.

"Wesley!" Leonore knew her voice was distorted and otherworldly as it resonated with the force of the power. She joined her mind with Liam's, and found his full of wonder and joy at the feel of the magic rushing through him. "Wesley!" she said again, and knew the moment when the king heard and took up the call.

"Wesley!" As she spoke the name a third time, this time in unison with Liam, she felt the blood on her hands and in the circle surrounding them surge and join the call. *Wesley!* Neither Leonore nor the king had said it aloud again, but the blood itself seemed to whisper. It called to its own and faintly, faintly, it seemed an answer was heard.

- *I am here*, said the voice, or would have if the faint response revealed to Leonore and, through their union, to the king, had truly been composed of words. *I am here, and I hear.*

"Tell us!" said Leonore and Liam, and the blood took up the words with its whispering chorus. *Tell us, show us, reveal to us. Tell us, show us, reveal to us.*

I am here, came again the faint response. Too faint—too far away. Leonore felt it struggle and waiver, as if unable to make its way through a thick fog. *I am here, and I hear.*

More power. We need more power. It cannot quite reach us. As soon as the thought entered Leonore's mind, she knew Liam perceived it as well. Again, she spoke aloud the words of ritual.

"*Amplio potentia! Cresco...augeo...incito...increbresco... ingemino!*"

The shimmering in the room increased and flashed as if miniature bolts of lightning shot around them. A great rush of wind seemed to swirl around them and the bed shook. Both of their bodies rose and snapped back as their remaining garments tore from them as if pulled by a cyclone.

"Wesley!" they shouted in unison, and the answering chorus of the blood was deafening to their ears. "Tell us! Show us! Reveal to us!"

I AM HERE! This time the response was not faint, but as powerful as a punch to the chest. Liam gasped, and Leonore redoubled her grip on his hands. Suddenly, the moving, liquid ball of power that roiled between them seemed to explode and fill the room with fragments like those of a shattered stained glass window. The fragments joined and shifted and coalesced into images. Leonore could not tell if the pictures danced before her eyes or only within her mind, but she could make them out clearly, even though they passed by with a swiftness that was dizzying.

A young man's face bathed in torchlight, the eyes wide with terror as a gloved hand covered his mouth and a burning bundle was placed before his nose. The same young man, limp and unconscious, thrown over a muscular shoulder and carried down a narrow stairs. The face of the man carrying him showed briefly in the light of a torch, but Leonore felt no recognition from Liam.

Next there were horses, and the still-limp form of a man being carried like a sack of grain. Strong arms lifting the man and forcing water into his mouth. A voice saying, "He will awaken soon. Hurry!" Stone steps leading down…the sound of an iron gate slamming shut. More voices…men arguing. A voice rising clearly above the clamor saying, "Enough! Keep him secure. I must get back to Liam's court and inform our lord we have been successful."

Now silence and cold stones. Wesley, awakening with a spinning head feeling sick…so sick. Leonore could feel the nausea as if roiled in her own stomach. And thirst. Leonore felt Liam's anger and frustration as if they were her own emotions, and his thoughts became her own and echoed in her mind.

"Who must he get back to? Who is his lord? Who at my court has done this thing?" Liam's voice spoke through her lips—through both their lips. All around them and in them, the blood resonated with the word, *Who? Who? Who?* and Leonore let the thought take her, as she poured all of her concentration into the question. *Who? Who? Who?*

The roiling crystal images swirled, broke, reformed. Colors danced and blue light hovered and crackled. Leonore felt her skin sting as something cold and wet fell like wasps' needles against her naked flesh. Gooseflesh covered her body and her nipples grew hard. The roiling power seemed to enter her body through the opening of her womanhood and shudder through her like an orgasm. Still the question beat in her mind like a relentless drum. *Who? Who? Who?*

Again, she was on the cold floor in the dark cell, feeling the pain in Wesley's head. The nausea had subsided, and the cold penetrated through the stone floor. A bolt shot back and the door flew open, bringing torchlight, blinding to Wesley's dark-accustomed eyes. The smell of food flooded Leonore's nostrils. "Who are you?" she croaked through Wesley's lips, in unison with Liam. "Why have you brought me here?"

"Because my lord ordered me to," was the curt reply, and again Leonore heard her own words asked in Wesley's and the king's voices at the same time.

"Who is your lord?" *Who? Who? Who?*

"Mellinor," came the answer, and the blood repeated. *Mellinor...Mellinor...Mellinor.*

Leonore felt the king's surprise and outrage as if the emotions originated in her own breast, but even stronger was the sensual beat of the power welling through her very pores. *Mellinor! Mellinor! Mellinor!*

With a great howl, King Liam rose almost to his feet on the shuddering bed. His hands slipped from Leonore's grasp and she gasped as the ball of power lengthened into a column and rushed upward to explode and vanish with a sound like a thunderclap.

The unbroken blood circle still pulsed and echoed, no longer with words that could be understood, but with a pounding that echoed in every pore of Leonore's body. With eyes suddenly clear of visions, she stared up into Liam's dark gaze. He stood above her, the rain that pelted sideways through the open window glistening in his beard as it was lit by a flash of lightning—real lightning this time and no byproduct of their spell. He breathed like a man who had run a long race and the veins stood out in his neck, chest and upper arms. Magic still crackled around him tangibly and his engorged cock stood fully erect, seeming to throb in time with the drumbeat that echoed from the blood circle.

With a cry, King Liam seized Leonore. There were no words, no caresses, no tenderness, only a searing animal need that washed through both of them like a tide. "Take me! Take me now!" she shrieked, and he did.

The king's shaft plunged into her waiting body like a shooting star torn from the sky, and she was ready for him. Wet and hot, she enveloped him like a creature devouring its prey. She screamed as he filled her, pounding her like a wave against a shore during the most violent of storms, and still it was not enough. "More!" she cried. "Deeper!" And the king, who Leonore knew could still hear her words inside her head as well as with his ears, did everything in his power to obey her command.

Again and again he plunged, and as the blood on her palms sang and danced in rhythm with their bodies and the song of the circle, she realized she was feeling not only her own orgasm, but the king's own rising tide, and his body began to clench and shudder in preparation for his own climax. She knew he felt her sensations as well, and as his body made its final spasms, their mingled screams rent the air. With one final thrust, they both fell on the tangled furs and sheets, panting for breath.

As the rain from the window washed away the blood circle, the drumbeats in Leonore's mind began to flicker and fade, and by the time her own heartbeat had slowed, they died entirely. The wind lost some of its strength, and the rain no longer came through the narrow window. Leonore could hear the sizzle of the charcoal in the brazier as the coals gave up the last of their fire to the rain's assault.

She lay with her head against Liam's chest, and soon his heartbeat slowed to a normal pace and his breath became regular. She lifted her head to look at him, and he did the same. Simultaneously, they laughed.

"For the first time since I've seen you, you look like a witch." He ran his fingers across her cheek and displayed them to Leonore. She saw the remains of both blood smears and blue daub on them.

"And you look like an ancient pagan god, with your hair wild and wet and blue in your beard. If Wallix and Chellasandre saw you right now, they would think they had accidentally conjured a demon and run screaming in fear." She drew herself up and looked around for her shift, expecting to find it in shreds. She saw it on the floor, luckily on the side of the bed sheltered from the rain, and leaned across the king to pick it up. She straightened and saw Liam had been looking appreciatively at her bare bottom.

"So, Your Majesty, was your first attempt at conjuring magic everything you had hoped?" she asked, and was rewarded with a warm smile.

"And more. He reached out and tweaked one still-erect nipple. "Much more than I expected. Did you know we would...that it would turn out this way?"

"I knew it might." She held out the shift and was surprised to find it relatively undamaged. Only one tie was broken. She pulled it over her head and began fastening the ties, which brought a sour expression to the King's face. "When we had to summon the additional power, every part of our bodies became involved in the ritual. One cannot help but be stimulated by the experience."

"Stimulated." Liam grinned. "You could certainly call it that."

A rush of footsteps was heard on the stairs, and a loud pounding came on the door, accompanied by Geoffrey's voice. "King Liam! Is everything all right? Chellasandre said she heard screams from the tower."

"Everything is fine," called Leonore. "We have just finished the ritual."

"We will open the door in a moment," added the king. "We are just...finishing up." Leonore, who had hopped from the bed at the first sound of footsteps, tossed the king his braies from where they had landed behind the bed. Putting them on, he stood and reached for his tunic.

Leonore tried to glimpse her reflection in the polished metal shield that Wesley apparently used as a mirror. The blue streaks she could do nothing about without soap and water, but she found a brush and ran it through her tangled curls. She tossed it to the king so he could do the same, then pulled her kirtle back over her head and fastened the girdle. Finally, she pulled her hair into a twist and thrust it down the back of her dress.

"How do I look?" she whispered to the king. She had not heard Geoffrey's footsteps retreat, and assumed he was waiting impatiently at the top of the stairs.

"Like a woman who has just conjured a spell and then been raped by a pagan god," whispered Liam in return, his white teeth flashing in the blue-streaked beard.

Leonore stifled a laugh and then started to reach for the door, but Liam stopped her. Silently, he pointed toward the bedclothes, which were streaked with red blood and blue daub, and in a sort of disarray that could only have been caused by one thing. Silently, she crossed to the other side of the bed, and between the two of them, the covers were pulled back to no worse a condition than before the ritual. Leonore retrieved the dagger and tucked it back into her kirtle, and was in the process of picking up the kettle, bowl and cup when the king opened the door.

"Are you well, Liam?" Leonore heard Geoffrey's voice from behind her as she replaced the kettle on the brazier. She supposed his use of the king's first name was a testament to his agitation at being unable to be present during the ritual. *It is a good thing he was not*, she thought to herself. *That could have been a really unusual experience.* Suppressing a smile, she turned in time to see the king put his hand on Geoffrey's shoulder.

"I am fine, Geoffrey. More than fine. The ritual was a complete success, would you not agree, Leonore?"

"Complete," she agreed, and was astonished to find herself blushing. *Why do I feel embarrassed in front of Geoffrey? I have done nothing of which to be ashamed.* She wondered if Geoffrey's sharp look meant he had guessed anything about what had happened at the rite's end.

"Let us get to my antechamber with all speed," said Liam. "It is late, and we know now who our enemy is and where he has taken Wesley. We have no time to waste." As full of energy as a youth at midmorning, the king rushed passed Geoffrey and flew down the stairs like a man who knew neither that his fiftieth birthday had passed, nor the two hours since midnight. Geoffrey looked after him in surprise then turned to Leonore.

"What happened here?" he asked, more with a tone of curiosity than suspicion.

Leonore found herself avoiding his eye. "As he said, the ritual was a success." She also swept past Geoffrey and began down the flight of stairs as he turned to follow. "We learned what we needed to know, and now he is ready to take action." He did not respond, and as Leonore continued down the long stairs, only the echoes of their footfalls and the sound of distant thunder could be heard in the sleeping castle.

Chapter Eight

ಐ

King Liam paced his antechamber in agitation. Geoffrey stifled a yawn and noticed Wilfred attempting to do the same, with somewhat less success. The king had awakened a page and sent him to rouse the most seasoned warrior in his employ. Geoffrey was glad of Wilfred's presence, no matter how much he grumbled. In fact, Liam had so far addressed most of his questions to Wilfred.

"So the stairs we saw in the vision lead down to a dungeon?"

"Aye, 'tis a massive thing." Wilfred ran his fingers through his sleep-wild mane of grey-streaked red hair. "Prisoners kept coming out of it like rats. Some had to be carried, and I went down to the first level and into a few of the cells." A shudder racked his frame. "'Twas horrible. But I did not see the whole thing—there were tunnels leading off in all directions. Of course, that was twelve years ago, Your Majesty. Mellinor may have filled them in, or let them fall into ruin."

Wilfred had ridden at Liam's side when he had joined with Mellinor, a neighboring baron, to rout the fort's previous occupant. This was a particularly troublesome man who had tried to set himself up as king, generally by killing or imprisoning anyone who did not agree wholeheartedly with his mostly imagined claims of lineage. As a reward, Liam had granted Mellinor some of the man's lands, including that on which the fort stood.

Geoffrey was more than a little uncomfortable with the fact that the king had apparently decided whatever he and Leonore had "seen" during whatever ritual they had performed was solid fact, and was ready to mount a rescue based on his perceptions. Leonore had been fairly quiet, other than to fill in a few details of the events she and King Liam both claimed to have witnessed.

Once Mellinor had been established as the culprit, they had narrowed down the possible sites of the cell they described to places owned or controlled by the king's supposed ally. Although he had never lived at the fort, having much more comfortable accommodations a distance away, Mellinor had dutifully kept a small contingent of armed men stationed there, to prevent brigands from taking up residence and causing trouble for the nearby roads and villages. As soon as this place had been named, its attributes had matched so well with Liam and Leonore's perception of Wesley's current surroundings that they had called for Wilfred to start planning in earnest.

Despite his doubts, Geoffrey chafed to mount an assault on the fort. At least he would be doing *something* to get the young prince back. If it turned out Wesley was not there, they could apologize to Mellinor and then…well, they would cross that bridge when they came to it. He decided it was time to voice his opinion.

"Last time I was by the fort, there could not have been more than two dozen men encamped. We could take them by surprise, get Wesley out, and be back in less than two days."

Liam shook his head. "No, Geoffrey, I do not want to launch an obvious attack unless there is no other option. First, having two score of my knights disappear in the middle of holding court would arouse a lot of talk. I have begun to make progress with some of the more difficult of the group, and if they learn one of my oldest allies has turned against me, they will take their men and go home—or join him openly and cause warfare within the very walls of the castle."

Liam waited for Geoffrey's nod of understanding to continue. "I want him out of there as soon as possible, but I want him whisked out of there as quietly as he was taken from here. I want him to walk into the main hall at midday, and sit down at my right hand and begin drinking his soup as if he had really just returned from the hunting trip I have told everyone he is on." King Liam's eyes glinted dangerously.

"And I most especially want to see the look on Mellinor's face when that happens. *And* when I let him know I wish to have a private word with him as soon as the meal is finished."

"I like the sound of that as well," said Wilfred. "Especially if I can be around during the 'private word'. But how are we going to get him out without raising any notice? For all we know, Mellinor has sent more men to the fort. He may have speculated we would eventually guess where Wesley is being held, and we could be riding into an ambush." To Geoffrey's irritation, Wilfred also seemed to have no reservations about basing assumptions of Wesley's whereabouts on a supposedly magical vision.

"Because *we* are going to be the ones setting up an ambush. And we are going to do it with so few men that no one will remark their absence." King Liam turned and spoke to Leonore. "And since almost no one knows Leonore is here, no one will notice her absence at meals, either."

Despite his fatigue, Geoffrey was on his feet. "You cannot be thinking to send a woman on a raid!"

"Not a woman, Sir Geoffrey. A witch." Liam smiled wickedly. "The bastards will never know what hit them."

* * * * *

He knows. Leonore had allowed her horse to drop slightly behind Geoffrey's, and was studying the set of his back and shoulders. They had left before daylight, and with very little sleep. Leonore did not require much sleep, at least not when her veins coursed with power, as they now did. She indulged herself by letting a small flow run through her limbs, enjoying the warm tingle. She had been feeling wonderful since her nights with Geoffrey. At the memory, a different tingle spread through her loins. As her nether regions tightened, she felt the horse react slightly to the corresponding flex of her inner thighs. "Sorry, my love," she murmured, patting the arched neck. "I was thinking of something else."

Yes, Geoffrey's sex had filled what she thought of as her ewer of power more fully than for many years. The brief coupling with Liam had not. Not that it had not also been enjoyable. Leonore smiled at the memory of the King's virility and his pure joy as magic coursed through him. But the ritual itself had taken much more power than the sex had restored. It was, regrettably, always the way with such magic.

Leonore looked again at Geoffrey's stiff posture. *His back will be sore if he rides much farther like that.* It had taken a great deal of argument before the noble knight had agreed to the king's plan, and he had not surrendered until Wilfred had voiced his approval. But it was not his reluctance about the mission that caused his ramrod posture, Leonore knew. It was jealously. Some time in the early part of the ride, when they were still passing through Liam's villages and farmlands and had to keep quiet, Geoffrey had apparently worked out that his king and Leonore had made more than magic in Wesley's tower room.

Why should I care if he is angry with me? Leonore had certainly dealt with jealous lovers before. She had simply told them to get over it. Gently, of course. On a few extreme occasions, she had even used magic to erase or fade their memories, in order to keep the peace.

But Leonore did not *want* Geoffrey to forget the intensity of their lovemaking. For one thing, she intended to bed him again, and sooner rather than later. For another...

She sighed deeply. For some reason, Leonore *did* care about Geoffrey's jealousy, or hurt feelings, or whatever it was that was making him sit on his horse as if tied to a scarecrow's pole. She urged her horse to regain her place at Geoffrey's side.

"Out with it," she said without preamble.

"Out with what?" he replied, jumping as if startled. Leonore was not fooled—a subtle change in his posture had told her he had heard her horse's approach.

"Out with whatever it is you want to say to me, but are too stubborn to voice."

"What gives you the idea there is something I want to talk about?" Geoffrey's eyes stayed on the trail ahead as he spoke, which was a good thing. Leonore had been unable to suppress a smile at his sanctimonious tone. He was probably trying to talk himself into believing she was a slut and not worth his notice. He was obviously failing miserably.

"It is quite obvious something has been on your mind since daylight," she continued, unperturbed. "And as you stiffen every time I draw near, I assume it has something to do with me." Leonore watched Geoffrey's muscles relax with a visible effort.

"I am just concerned about this plan to use magic to rescue Wesley," he said. "I am not comfortable with it."

"You made that abundantly clear back at the castle, but I do not believe that is the only thing bothering you." When Geoffrey looked at her sharply, Leonore continued, "You have been a leader of men for a number of years, Geoffrey. If you wanted to discuss a matter of strategy, you would simply do so. This is something else, and it is something more...personal."

When Geoffrey's silence continued, Leonore lost patience. "Oh, for the sake of the goddess!" she said. "We are about to go into a dangerous situation where we will have to count on one another. If there is something affecting your feelings toward me, we need to get it out of the way now and be done with it."

At her tone, Geoffrey finally gave her his full regard. "All right, I will tell you. It is about this magical rite you performed with Liam." He paused, seemingly unsure about how to continue.

"What about it?" she prompted.

"You did not tell me beforehand you would…that he…that the two of you…"

Leonore was not going to rescue him by finishing his sentence. "Did not tell you we would *what*?"

"You did not say the two of you would make love!" The words came out in a burst, and Geoffrey's face flushed as he turned his gaze back to the rode ahead.

"I assure you, Geoffrey, what Liam and I did had little to do with love. It was sex, pure and simple."

"Like you had with me?" Geoffrey countered quickly.

"Not in the least." Leonore chose her words carefully. "I have told you my power is strengthened by the pleasure I receive during sex."

"You told me." Geoffrey's reply was terse.

"Well, there is a great deal more to it than that. My power often manifests itself in a highly sensual and arousing manner. The ritual King Liam and I performed…well, it required we blend our energy and our minds. The power was in *both* of us. He could feel what I was feeling, and I could feel him as well."

While Geoffrey's brows were still beetled, he now showed signs of interest amidst the consternation. "You mean you could feel his…member? I mean what it felt like to him?"

"Yes. And he could feel what I was experiencing as well." Leonore saw Geoffrey was considering the implications of this statement, and hastened to use this slight shift to her advantage. "The ritual does not always require that level of intensity to be reached in order to be effective. I truly did not know ahead of time if it would come to that."

"But you knew it might." Leonore could no longer read Geoffrey's expression.

"Yes."

"And the reason you did not mention this ahead of time?"

"Because..." Leonore paused, considering her answer. *Because it never mattered before. Why did it matter this time?* She modified her answer. "I am not accustomed to explaining every potential outcome of my magic ahead of time. It did not occur to me to do so this time." That was honest enough.

Geoffrey nodded. "I see." He seemed to make up his mind about something. "Well, I suppose I should not have expected it. I apologize if I have been ungracious about it."

Leonore looked at him carefully. His relaxed posture no longer seemed forced. Did this mean he had forgiven her?

"Geoffrey, you have nothing for which to apologize. I had not considered you are not a man who appreciates or understands magic. I will attempt to be more forthcoming in the future."

"It is not necessary."

"No, but it takes little effort on my part to do so." She tried an experimental smile with him, to see if he would respond in kind. He did not, and she continued. "I admit to deriving a certain amount of personal satisfaction from keeping my talents mysterious. It is a vanity, and I am a vain woman."

This last finally drew a smile from Geoffrey, albeit a small one. "Leonore, you may rest assured you are still a complete mystery to me." This said, he urged his horse forward in order to go single file on the suddenly narrowing path. Apparently he had decided the conversation was at an end. But Leonore was pleased to see he now sat on the horse with his accustomed ease.

* * * * *

Geoffrey peered through the trees at the fort beyond. "Those palisades are new," he observed. The shadows grew long, but it was still light enough to see the wooden fence had not yet darkened to the color of weathered timber.

"Aye," agreed Wilfred. "Now why do you think Mellinor thought he needed a barricade so badly he could not wait to repair the old stone wall?"

Knowing Wilfred did not really expect an answer to this question, Geoffrey motioned to Leonore. As instructed, she crawled to the edge of the trees and peered through the spot Geoffrey indicated.

"Is there a gate?" she asked after a moment. "In the palisade, I mean."

"If there is, it is not closed." Wilfred squinted, but Geoffrey had already determined the inner postern was hidden from their current position. "The main gate will be closed, though."

· "There is no portcullis, or at least there was not last time we were here." Geoffrey was still trying to assess the viability of a frontal assault.

"It should not matter," retorted Leonore. "I am going to send men out to meet *you*, not the other way around. You should not have to enter the fort at all."

Geoffrey turned to look at her. "You are very confident."

"Of some things." Having apparently seen enough, she backed away from the clearing's edge. Geoffrey and Wilfred followed her example, and the trio moved quietly back to where the rest of their small party waited with the horses.

"Are there things about which you are *not* confident?" Geoffrey did not want to start another argument about the wisdom of including Leonore in the rescue party—King Liam had already firmly overruled him on this point—but he was still the nominal leader of the mission, and wanted to know every detail.

"I believe there are a lot more men in the fort than we originally guessed," said Leonore. "Before we left the road, I was beginning to get a sense it was very heavily traveled, and ever more so as we got closer to the fort."

"What kind of sense?" To Geoffrey's annoyance, Wilfred sounded more curious than skeptical.

"Oh, nothing specific," said Leonore. "It was just not as quiet as I expected."

"Do you mean you heard something, and did not tell us?" Geoffrey heard the annoyance creep into his voice.

"No, nothing like that." Leonore sighed. "Let me see if I can explain." She took a few moments, as if to gather her thoughts. "Have you ever been traveling alone, and come to a place where you could just tell...just *feel* you were the first person to stand there in countless years? Or looked at a mountain or a lake, and somehow just known if your great-grandfather had seen the same sight, it would have been exactly the same?"

Geoffrey was about to scoff at the idea, but was interrupted by Wilfred. "Aye. You get the feeling if you were to speak, your voice would...would break something. Like it does not belong there."

"Exactly." Leonore beamed at Wilfred, and the old dog beamed back like a student who had answered a tutor's difficult question. "And when you do speak, the feeling changes. It is no longer so untouched and pure." Wilfred nodded eagerly, and Geoffrey resisted the impulse to point out Leonore should be the last one to talk about things being *untouched* or *pure*.

"If you become very sensitive to the changes a human's presence makes to a place, just by passing through it, you can sometimes tell how recently a place has been visited, and by how many people." She turned her attention to Geoffrey. "The road felt normal for most of the way. It was more heavily traveled near the villages and, of course, the castle. Then it got quiet. But when we got closer to the fort, it got, well...louder again. Full of the unquiet thoughts of men who are expecting trouble, or had been warned against it."

Geoffrey wanted to argue, but he realized it did not really matter how Leonore came by this theory. The possibility the fort was heavily manned was real, and had to be considered. "So does this mean you are no longer confident of your part of the plan?"

"Not at all," she replied. "My part is to gain entry to the fort and get Wesley out. The number of men in the fort should not change my chances of success at all." This statement made no sense to Geoffrey, but he decided to humor her.

"So what, Leonore, concerns you?"

"Well, although my chances of failure are still small, they have never been nonexistent. It is *your* chances that may be affected." Geoffrey could no longer suppress his incredulity at her vanity.

"So you, a single woman, could as easily handle a hundred men as a dozen, but my twelve seasoned fighting men are likely to be defeated by too large a force?"

"If it is a large enough force, yes." Leonore wrinkled her brow. "I will just have to make doubly sure it does not come to that."

"Explain to me, Leonore, just how you plan to do that." Geoffrey folded his arms over his chest and gave her his best skeptical look.

"Well, I will have to determine the number of men in the fort immediately, before I tell my tale."

"Why?"

"So I know how many bandits attacked me."

Geoffrey wanted to argue, but immediately saw Leonore's point. The plan required her to entice a party of men into leaving the fort in order to pursue a fictional band of highwaymen. If she said there were too few bandits, they might decide only one or two soldiers would be needed for the pursuit. If she said it was too large, they might send out more men than Geoffrey's trap could handle. However many men stayed behind at the fort, that was how many she would have to overcome with her magic.

"How many men can you handle with your enchantment?" he asked.

"As many as I have to, but more will take longer. That is not the problem. It is that in the unlikely event I fail to make the rendezvous and you attack, you will have a larger force to deal with. And I will have no way of telling you just how large a force."

"I see." Geoffrey considered. "What do you think, Wilfred?"

Wilfred paused to give the matter thought. "I suppose they will be trained soldiers, and will believe their opponents to be unschooled ruffians. They will probably think they do not need to match the opponent's numbers."

"We will have surprise in our favor," added Geoffrey, "but we cannot afford to let even one man get back to the fort to warn the others. As you say, they will be trained fighters. We should not want to take on more than six or eight."

Wilfred nodded in agreement. "So you should tell them there were fewer than ten bandits. Nine sounds about right, I think."

"Unless there are fewer than six or eight men there. They will not want to leave me alone, or leave the prince unguarded," said Leonore. She slowed her pace, and Geoffrey saw they were almost back to where the rest of the troop waited. "Geoffrey, I would speak with you alone for a moment." Geoffrey motioned for Wilfred to rejoin the others, and changed directions to follow Leonore.

They walked a few paces into the forest, which was rapidly growing dimmer with the approach of twilight. When they were well out of hearing of the rest of the group, she sat on a fallen tree and motioned for Geoffrey to sit next to her. After a moment's hesitation, he complied.

"Geoffrey, I do not like the idea that we will be parted tonight with a misunderstanding between us," she said.

"There is no misunderstanding. You had sex with the king. It was part of a ritual." Geoffrey squelched the resentment he felt returning before it could fully form. "I had no right or reason to question you about it. We have already settled the matter."

"Yes, well…" Leonore seemed at a loss for words, and Geoffrey thought he saw a flush steal across her face in the twilight. "Geoffrey, I told you before that I was unaccustomed to explaining myself."

"You have no need to explain yourself to me, Leonore."

"Perhaps not." Leonore shifted on the log to face him and took his hand. "But I find, to my own very great surprise, I wish to do so." She smiled gently, and Geoffrey felt the sudden hard pulse of his arousal. He shifted uncomfortably, and if Leonore noticed she made no sign.

"When the ritual with Liam reached its…natural conclusion, I did not feel I had done anything wrong. But the moment I heard your voice at the door, I realized I did not want you to know what happened." She squeezed the hand she was holding. "I have had many lovers, and have grown exceedingly fond of some of them. But never before have I worried one of them might not…might not respect me. Nor cared."

The sound of her voice and the pressure of her hand combined to make Geoffrey's head swim as it had the first time she had touched him. He struggled to control his ardor, because he knew her words held great import. His body, however, was rebelling. Her scent—it was the springtime scent he had first experienced in her bed. He willed himself to hold still until she had finished speaking.

"I realize now I did not want you to think less of me because I had lain with another man so soon after our own lovemaking. Because I find you are someone whose opinion I care about. And also," she put one of her hands on his cheek and leaned forward to place the other on this thigh, "because I very much want to be with you in that way again. As soon as may be."

Geoffrey groaned aloud as the pressure of her hand and nearness made his pulse increase yet again, and the fullness of his growing erection pressed against his trousers. "Leonore, if you do not stop, it will be in the next few moments."

"And why should it not be?" Her tone changed to a husky purr as she shifted her hand to caress the evidence of his arousal through his trousers.

"Leonore, we cannot do this here," he gasped. "It grows dark, and the men are waiting."

"They must wait until full dark to move to the ambush site," she reminded him. Now both hands worked at the laces of his trousers, and he was about to reply when his swollen staff sprang free into her waiting hands. "We will be back in plenty of time."

"Leonore, we—" Geoffrey's words were cut off by a moan as Leonore dipped her head, took the engorged head of his rod between her lips and began to tease it with her tongue.

"Ummm…the skin is so smooth." Her flickering tongue stopped long enough for her to speak before he felt it dance down the length of his member and up again, before she once again engulfed the head with her mouth. She sucked gently, sliding off the fallen tree and pivoting to kneel before him.

No longer capable of arguing, Geoffrey leaned back and let her pleasure him. Her mouth was a wonder—soft yet strong. She let her teeth graze him in a tantalizing brush, but instantly replaced them with her slithering tongue and soft lips. She began to move rhythmically, pulling him deeper into her mouth then out toward her lips so he could feel the head of his cock being drawn into the swelling of her throat, then pulled away. He knew such pleasure would soon culminate in a release of his seed, when suddenly the pressure ceased.

He opened his eyes to see Leonore rising to her feet, pulling her skirts up as she climbed upon his legs. She wore nothing under her shift and in moments he felt himself plunged into the fiery furnace between her thighs.

Joined together, they rocked on the log, Geoffrey holding on to Leonore's body to avoid falling as she braced herself against the remnants of branches jutting from the tree's trunk. She managed to lift her buttocks up and down at the same time, so his shaft slid in and out of her hot, slick core even as she rode him so it plunged deep, deep into her. He felt his testicles pull up and would have cried out, forgetting the nearness of the men, when her mouth closed over his and swallowed his scream. Her body gripped him tightly, seeming to pull and squeeze the seed out of him. His climax went on and on, and he had to pull his mouth away from hers to breathe.

Leonore's head was thrown back, and he could barely make out the passion on her face that must mirror his own. Her body bucked and shuddered as it echoed the final spasms of his frenzied release. Her eyes opened, and Geoffrey thought he could just make out a glint of green fire as the final light faded into the forest's gloom.

Chapter Nine

෨

Leonore winced as her fingers gingerly probed the bruise on her cheek. She hoped it was starting to darken. Geoffrey had been reluctant to hit her, but she had patiently explained a bruise or two would be of great help in convincing the fort's occupants she had indeed been attacked. It was only when she threatened to ask Wilfred to hit her instead that he had agreed.

She smiled, remembering Geoffrey's horrified expression in the moonlight when he realized he had split her lip. It really had hurt, but she had assured him it did not. She tugged at the torn shoulder of her kirtle to make sure her shoulder was exposed. Geoffrey had not had to be asked to provide that particular detail—it had happened when she mounted him as he sat on the fallen tree. Her nether regions still tingled from their lovemaking. The scrapes on her hands were also real, from when she had grasped the rough tree-bark to keep from falling as she rode the bucking knight. All that had been needed to complete the disguise was a little dirt—her hair was already disheveled—and she was the perfect picture of a distressed noblewoman.

She threaded her way carefully around the palisades in the intermittent moonlight, looking for the guards who must surely be watching the fort's outermost defenses. Finally, she heard the soft murmuring of voices near a copse of trees, and drew closer to make out two shapes standing in the shadows. *Lazy idiots.* No doubt they had been ordered to guard different sections of the fort's boundaries, but had grown bored and gotten together for a little talk. And with so many hours until daylight.

Leonore doubled back to the other side of the fence, making a wide arc so she could approach as if happening upon the barrier while running away from the forest nearest the road. She took a deep breath to prepare then made herself pant as if from exertion and terror. She began an uneven, staggering run toward the fence, pleased when the clouds overhead moved and exposed her to a brilliant beam of moonlight. Through eyes made deliberately wild and darting, she noticed when both shade-shrouded figures stiffened and turned toward her.

Leonore staggered again and fell to her knees, letting out a stifled sob. She made a great show of tripping over her skirts as she struggled to regain her feet. She heard feet pounding toward her and voices as the two men scaled the fence rather than running around to the gate. *Good,* she thought, then frowned as she saw from their silhouettes that both men had drawn their swords as soon as they had cleared the fence. She had better let them hear a feminine voice before they stabbed her in the dark.

She fell again then looked toward the two running figures. "Help me!" she gasped. "Oh, please save me before they catch me again!" She was pleased to see them pause when they heard her voice, then rush over with their swords hanging at their sides rather than in a position of readiness.

"What is it?" said one. "What has happened? Who are you?"

"Oh, thank God, thank God," she sobbed, rising to her knees and throwing herself against the first man's legs. Startled, he dropped his sword and attempted to catch her.

"What in hell..." The other man came alongside and stopped in confusion. "Who are you and what are you doing here?"

"They attacked us!" she said, still sobbing. "They killed my husband and our guards and took all my jewelry..." She erupted in a paroxysm of wails and clawed at the two men as if trying to rise. "Please, they have my daughter! They will kill her after they...after they..." As hands reached out to lift her, she collapsed neatly into one of the men's arms and went limp.

"She's fainted," said the man in astonished tones.

"We'd better get her inside," said the other. "Lorance will know what to do with her. Get my sword." The taller of the two men gathered Leonore up and began to carry her, and the other man caught up in a few steps.

"Where do you think she came from?" asked the man who was not carrying her. "It sounds like highwaymen attacked her party."

"Aye, they must have been along the road somewhere. I wonder how she got away."

"Is she wounded, do you think?"

"Won't know until we get her inside." The larger man was beginning to flag a bit under Leonore's weight, but she kept herself limp. As long as she was being taken inside the fort, she did not want to impede progress.

She heard the sounds of their footfalls change from the soft thuds of grass-covered grounds to the ring of cut stones. Other voices could be heard fairly nearby and, finally, the shout of alarm she had expected.

"Who goes there?" said one voice, to be immediately interrupted by another.

"It's Jame and Merfyd, and they're carrying someone."

"'Tis a lady," said the much closer voice of the sword carrier. "She's fainted. She says she was attacked." Leonore felt the warmth of a torch being brought near her face, and allowed her eyes to flutter open.

"Help me," she said faintly, keeping her gaze deliberately unfocused. "They have my daughter..." She rolled her eyes back in her head and let her head loll back.

A cacophony of voices erupted around Leonore, punctuated with cries of, "This way," and "Get the door," and the like. She was being carried up a short flight of stairs when she noted a few voices saying, "Get Lorance," which boded well for her plan. Leonore had intended to ask to see whoever was in charge, but it appeared she was being taken directly to just such a person.

As the now-panting man set her down onto some sort of bench or sofa, she again began fluttering her lashes. She was in a much warmer room, and not a large one, and too many men were trying to crowd in. "Where—" she began, and a chorus of voices answered her.

"At the fort of Greenwald," said one.

"In the captain of the guard's room," said another, pleasing Leonore.

"Please..." she said. "Please, you must go after them. They took my daughter. They were after the gold."

"Gold?" As Leonore had hope, this word had apparently caught several sets of ears. A disturbance at the edge of the crowd heralded the arrival of Lorance.

"Stand aside!" thundered a deep, coarse voice. "Let me see her." The heads above Leonore parted, and she saw a large red face surrounded by a bushy black beard appear. His heavy brows furrowed in consternation. "What have we here?" he said, gruffly but not angrily. "A pretty picture, I think." His dark eyes raked up and down her form, pausing on her heaving bosom, somewhat more exposed than usual by the torn dress.

"Please..." Leonore began again, and put her arms to her side as if struggling to rise to a sitting position. Several hands reached out to help her, and she was soon more or less upright. "Thank you," she said, looking around at her rescuers with tear-filled eyes. "You are being too kind." She was gratified by several blushes and mumbled assurances as she turned to face the enormous red-faced man.

"Please, you must help me," she said. "My husband and I were on our way to pay tribute to the High King," this caused the man's eyebrows to rise, but he nodded for her to continue, "when we were attacked by brigands. They carried off my daughter and k-k-killed my poor husband..." Leonore allowed herself a light sob before visibly marshalling her courage to continue. "They took me, too, but after they...after they were done with me and were...were looking to my daughter, I got away and ran to the road."

Lower lip trembling, she looked up at the man appealingly. "I abandoned her to those...those *animals*, but I could not stop them and I thought if I could get some help..." Again, she was overcome by sobs.

"Ask her about the gold, sir," said one of the onlookers, and Lorance glanced at him sharply.

"What about gold?" he said, and Leonore resumed her speech.

"That must be why they attacked us. My husband was making a gift of gold to the king, and jewels for his new bride as well. They must have heard of it. They took my jewels as well, and my clothes, and our horses..."

"You traveled with no guards?" Lorance seemed very interested in her story now.

"Two, and they fought bravely, but they were no match for eight men.

"Eight, you say."

"I think so. Or maybe nine, although some of them seemed mere boys."

The men all began muttering among themselves. Leonore heard several mentions of gold, jewels and even "young girl" before Lorance silenced them.

"Do you know where they are now?" asked Lorance.

"Not far, I do not think." Leonore was careful to be vague—a recently ravished noblewoman would be confused about a night flight through unfamiliar woodlands. "They camped just barely out of sight of the road. There was a big turn, I think, right after I found it, and I followed it all the way here. It seemed like forever but," she ventured a trembling smile, "I do not imagine I really came very far."

"Which way did she come from?" Lorance faced the crowd, and Leonore's two "rescuers" piped up. "From the south, sir. They must be camped just past where it bends to go around the ravine."

"They may be looking for her by now," said Lorance.

"Oh, I doubt it," said Leonore quickly, causing Lorance to return his gaze to her. "They found the wine we were taking to His Majesty, you see, and were drinking it like water."

"Let us go get them, captain, before they sober up," said the man who had carried Leonore into the room, and other voices joined in their assent.

"Ye cannot all go!" shouted Lorance, silencing the mêlée. "Mellinor will have my head if I leave the place unguarded." He turned to Leonore. "Eight or nine and no more. You are sure?"

"I am quite sure," said Leonore. "I was counting them to keep my mind off…off what was happening."

"Were they on horseback?"

"No, although they stole our horses. But they did not have horses of their own before that, and I think some of ours ran off." The big man nodded then turned to his men.

"You, you and you." He began pointing to men one at a time, picking out what looked like six to Leonore. "Go get your horses ready. Tell Griffin to get mine ready as well. Jame, Merfyd, get back to your posts. I will be down in a moment to lead the party. The rest of you, back to your duties."

The men obeyed amid general mumbling. Leonore tried to surreptitiously count them, but they had not all fit into the room and she could not tell how many were standing on the stairs beyond, or had not known about her arrival and come at all. Certainly there had been more than the two dozen that Geoffrey had estimated. Lorance crouched down next to her.

"Now, let us talk about this camp." Lorance questioned her closely while she described the details of the layout of the fictitious camp. She was careful to give him enough information to make him confident it would be an easy task to kill the bandits and take the booty for himself, while retaining enough vagueness to support her role as someone distressed to the point of shock. When at last he seemed satisfied he had gleaned all the information he could, he stood.

"You may rest here. I will send someone in with water and wine." He stalked out without another word, leaving Leonore alone in the overheated room.

* * * * *

Leonore stood near the closed door, listening for footfalls in the hallway or on the stairs. She could barely hear the sounds of the departing search party, and wanted to be sure they were gone before she ventured farther.

I still do not know how many men remain in the fort. She took a calming breath. It was just one of the many steps she must accomplish, and quickly. She mentally ticked off the items on her list. First, she had to get the information she needed. It would simplify things greatly if the person Lorance was sending with water knew the answers to her questions—a simple glamour should suffice. Then—

Leonore's thoughts were interrupted by the sound of someone coming up the hall. The door opened and a young woman entered, escorted by an armed guard.

"I've brought ye water and wine," said the woman, setting down a tray. "And Lorance asked me to see if ye needed aught help with…" The woman gestured vaguely in the direction of Leonore's abdomen, causing Leonore to suppress a smile. Lorance believed her to have been raped, as she had intended. She was surprised he had thought to send a woman to see to her wellbeing. Unless Leonore had gauged his reactions incorrectly, he probably intended to take her himself, after he got back from collecting the gold, jewels and horses from the bandits. And the other, younger girl with which to disport, of course.

"Thank you," she said. "If you will both just look at my eyes..." Both faces swiveled up curiously, no doubt believing Leonore wanted to point out an injury. Instead, they both became slack-jawed and stared as Leonore conjured the glamour she had begun to gather at the first sound of their footfalls.

"You wish to answer my questions," she said, her voice sounding eerie even to her own ears. Both listeners nodded.

"How many men and women are staying here at the fort?" The lack of an immediate answer was, Leonore knew, only because they were mentally calculating.

"Forty men and one woman," said the guard, causing the woman to shake her head slightly.

"Forty-one men," she corrected. "And two women, counting you." The man frowned but did not contradict her.

"Does that include the men who went out to find the thieves?"

"Yes." This time the answer was simultaneous.

"And is there someone being kept prisoner here?"

"Yes." Again, the two spoke in unison.

"Do you know the prisoner's identity?"

"No," said the man, at the same time the woman said, "Yes."

"Who is the prisoner?"

"Prince Wesley," said the woman. Even in his entranced state, the guard's face took on an expression of surprise. Leonore wondered why the woman knew the captive's identity and the guard did not, but dismissed this as unimportant.

"Can you tell me where he is being kept?"

"Yes." This time there was no disagreement—apparently the prince's location was no secret.

"Tell me how to find him." When both voices started to speak at once, she corrected herself. "Stop! You, guard, sit down on that bench, please. And do not speak." The guard complied, and Leonore turned to face the woman."

"Begin again, and tell me how to find Prince Wesley, starting from this room."

"Go down the stairs and you will see a passage on your left. There is an iron door. Go through the door—"

"Will it be locked or guarded?" Leonore interrupted.

"Yes."

"Which one—locked or guarded?"

"Locked *and* guarded."

Leonore swore. "Who has the keys?"

"I have them." This surprised Leonore greatly, but she was not about to argue with good fortune. "Give them to me." The woman complied, removing a ring with several keys from a deep pocket in her apron.

"What happens after I go through the door?"

"You will be in the chamber of the guard."

Leonore reminded herself not to become frustrated with the literal and succinct answers normal for a person in a glamour-induced trance.

"Once I am in the chamber, how should I proceed in order to reach Wesley?"

"You will take the passage on the right. His cell is there."

"On the right-hand passage? How will I know which cell?"

"There is only one."

Leonore nodded. She was about to proceed when she realized she had forgotten an important matter. "How many guards are stationed outside tonight?"

"I do not know." Leonore glanced at the man who was seated as she had instructed. His face held an odd expression, which at first puzzled Leonore, then caused her to grin when she realized she had given him two conflicting orders. She had told him he wanted to answer her questions then bade him to be silent. He was fairly bursting to speak, and not being permitted to do so. She turned back to the woman."

"Thank you. You may sit down and rest now." The woman obeyed immediately, and Leonore went to stand in front of the guard.

"You may now tell me how many men are on guard outside of the walls of the fort."

As if a bottle stopper had been pulled, the man's answer rushed out of his mouth. "There are four, two in the front near the forest and one on either side of the hill in the rear."

"Thank you. You may rest now." The man slumped slightly, looking very peaceful. Leonore considered what she had learned. Forty men—Leonore assumed the woman had included Wesley in her count—minus the seven who had gone out still left thirty-three armed men. This presented two difficulties.

Despite what she had told Geoffrey, she could not simultaneously enchant thirty-three men. She would have to do it in smaller groups, and by the time she had cast her spell on the final men, the amount of time left before the first group began to recover would grow short. She would have to get Wesley out of the fort and to the rendezvous point very quickly—perhaps arriving there before Geoffrey and his men had even had time to deal with the party of seven she had sent into his ambush.

The two she held in front of her were held in no more than the thrall of the glamour, and would come to their senses as soon as she let the glamour recede or left their presence. They must be among the first group she placed under her spell, and it would be better if she could deal with as few groups as possible. She returned to stand in front of the guard.

"You will tell me where each man who is inside the fort is likely to be at this moment."

"I am here in Lorance's room. Bregold is in the kitchen. Gregor is in the kitchen. Melfrys…"

"Stop." said Leonore, fighting frustration. She had to be careful how she worded her questions, as her request for *each man* was apparently going to produce a name by name list. She thought a moment, then resumed.

"Tell me each *place* in the castle where men may be at this time, and how many men are likely to be there."

"One man is in Lorance's office," he said. "Three men are in the kitchen." He paused, but Leonore did not interrupt, as he seemed to be counting on his fingers. "About fifteen men are in the sleeping rooms and about five in the chamber of the guard."

"Where are the sleeping rooms?" interrupted Leonore.

"They are next to the chamber of the guard."

Leonore smiled, pleased at this news — it meant twenty of the men were in approximately the same place. She realized her interruption had stopped the guard's speech, and he looked ready to burst again. "Please go on telling me where the men are."

"One man is on guard outside the prisoner's cell." To Leonore's surprise, the narrative stopped. She counted on her fingers. Seven men in the raiding party, four on guard outside the fort, twenty in the chamber of the guard or thereabouts, one on guard duty, three in the kitchen, one before her. Oh, and Wesley in his cell. There were four men unaccounted for. Perhaps this man did not know where they were.

"Are there men whose location you do not know?" she asked him.

"No."

Leonore wondered how else to phrase the question to get the answer she sought. She turned to the woman.

"Besides the men we have talked about, are there others?" When this got no answer, Leonore felt her temper begin to flare. *Careful, or you will lose control of the glamour.* She tried again. "Besides the men in the posse, the men on guard outside the palisades, and the men inside the fort, are there other men?"

"Yes," said her two educators simultaneously. Leonore breathed a sigh of relief. "Where are they?"

"In the stables," was the chorused response.

"Ah." Leonore frowned. She did not want to take the time to go outside and round up men from hither and yon, but she did not want anyone to wander in while she was leading Wesley out through the front door. "What are they doing in the stables?"

"Taking care of the horses," said the guard, at the same time as the woman said, "Sleeping." Leonore nodded — it made sense some men would sleep in the stables to guard horses, and these same men would be in charge of their care. It did not mean none of them would come wandering into the kitchen in search of something to eat, or to seek out a friend in the guard room.

Leonore had to make a decision. She had thought to leave the outside guards alone, deciding the risk that one would enter the house was small enough to avoid the time it would take to find them and cast her spell. If she ran into one of them on her way to the rendezvous, a simple glamour would keep them quiet long enough to tie them up or knock them out. But eight men outside the walls, and four of them not on a required shift — that was a much greater risk. Should she take the time to find them?

Out of the corner of her eye, Leonore saw her two subjects, seated side by side on the bench, were blinking and looking at one another curiously. *Damn*, she thought, and returned her concentration to the glamour. Immediately, the pair's expressions returned to the placid stares of a few moments before. *Whatever I do, I had better do it immediately.* Uncertainty was not something Leonore commonly experienced, and she did not much like the sensation.

Careful not to let the glamour waver, she lifted her skirt and removed a bundle she had tied to her undergarments. Unfolding the small cloth, she exposed the powder she had prepared before leaving the castle and laid it on the tray next to the water and wine Lorance had so conveniently provided.

Abruptly, Leonore made her decision. Even though it would give her less time to get Wesley out of the fort, she could not leave the men in the stables to chance. "You two, please stand up." As the man and woman rose, she had a final thought about their disposition. One woman in a fort full of men...what if she was being kept her against her will? She addressed the woman.

"Why are you here at the fort?"

"I am here with my husband, Lorance," was the nearly toneless reply. Leonore reflected this did not necessarily mean she was a willing resident, but it was unlikely she was a prisoner.

"Is he a good man?"

"Better than some," the woman replied after some hesitation. Leonore could not help but smile — the trance-induced honesty could sometimes be amusing.

"Pick up the tray, please. Is there a way to get to the stables without passing any other men on the way?"

"Yes," said both voices.

"Then lead me to the stables by that route." The woman and man turned silently and left the room, and Leonore followed. They went down a flight of stairs and turned right — Leonore remembered the chamber of the guard was to the left — and came almost immediately to a wooden door. Being careful enough to stay in her charges' peripheral vision and to maintain the glamour, she accompanied them past another closed door and through a large croft to a stable that was built of the same new wood as the palisades. *A recent addition,* thought Leonore. Without pausing, her guides walked around to a large entrance, flung open to the mild evening. Torches lit the entrance, and several men were seated inside around a small brazier.

"Stand over by that open stall and wait for my command," she said quietly, and the pair did as bidden. Startled faces looked up, but there was more curiosity than hostility in the expression of the men.

"Farnum, what is going..." said one voice, which halted immediately as he met Leonore's eyes and his face became slack. One by one, the puzzled gazes came to rest upon Leonore's face and expressions quieted. Leonore counted silently as she intensified the glamour to encompass the larger group. She felt relief flood through her when the count reached eight, including her two escorts.

"You wish to answer my questions," she began, and eight faces looked at her with anticipation. "Are any of you supposed to be on guard duty?"

"Yes" and "Aye" came from a couple mouths at once.

"Please raise your hand if you are supposed to be on guard duty." Two hands rose and Leonore nodded. This was excellent luck, and about time.

"You, bring the tray before me." The woman stepped to stand before Leonore and hold the tray. Leonore was tiring of the split concentration required to hold the glamour, but she would have to continue for a few moments longer.

She opened the packet of powder and took a generous pinch with the fingers of her right hand. Taking the cup of water in her left—wine would be better, but she would save it for the larger group in the guard chamber—she spoke again to the woman. "Place the tray carefully on the bench and return to your place." As her orders were followed, Leonore took a step back so she could easily see all faces in the group. "Those who are standing, please sit down."

Leonore held the powder above the water and spoke in the ringing tones of the spell.

"*Dormio…quiesco…somnus…sopor…requietum…sileo…delec tatio…incuditas…dormio…quiesco…somnus.*" She released the powder into the cup as she spoke. Pulling the power of the glamour inward, she took a sip from the cup then held it aloft.

"*Dormio…quiesco…somnus…sopor…requietum…sileo…delec tatio…incuditas…dormio…quiesco…somnus.*" Almost instantly, everyone before her slumped and slid to the floor. Beatific smiles appeared on every face, and sighs of pleasure chorused eerily as the entire group sank into blissful dreams of sensual and erotic pleasure.

It is too bad they will remember very little, thought Leonore as she released the power with a shiver. She stretched, taut from holding the glamour for so long. Then she busied herself with the tray as she prepared to make her way to the door next to the croft, which was undoubtedly the kitchen. She suppressed a giggle as some of the soft sighs turned to moans. *It will probably be the best sexual experience some of them will ever have.*

Chapter Ten

ೞ

"Wesley!" Leonore called the name again as she tried yet another key in the lock. Could the woman have been mistaken about which cell contained the prisoner? "Are you in there?" Finally she heard a soft moan, and breathed a sigh of relief, followed by a moment of alarm. *Surely the sleeping spell could not have reached him here!* She cursed under her breath as the key failed to turn the lock. Had that been the last one? They all looked so much alike. She wished she knew a magical spell to open a locked door. There probably was such a thing, but she had never had need of it.

"Wesley, are you awake? Your father sent me to get you out." Another groan floated around the windowless door, and she thought it sounded more like its originator was trying to speak. Leonore calmed her thrumming nerves. Between four glamours, three sleeping spells and a near disaster when someone had wandered into the kitchen when she had been collecting her tray, nearly upsetting it and losing the last of the precious powder, she felt frayed.

Click. Leonore breathed a sigh of relief as a key she was almost sure she had already tried turned the heavy lock. "I'm coming in, Wesley." She placed her shoulder against the door and pushed, causing the hinges to emit tortured shrieks. There was no reaction from the moaning and twitching guards, but Leonore had not expected any.

"Wesley?" Another groan sounded from the cell, but Leonore could not see its source in the dark interior. Putting the keys back in her pocket, she retrieved the torch from the wall sconce where she had placed it when struggling with the door. Holding it before her, she entered the gloom.

The cell was as she had seen it in her vision, the floor of stone and the walls glistening with moisture. A heap of something stirred near the back wall. "Who...?" came a feeble voice, and Leonore saw a trembling, white hand raised as if to shield its owner from the light.

"Wesley!" Immediately, Leonore stepped forward and put the torch into a notch in the stone wall made for the purpose. "You must come with me. Your father has sent me to get you out." She reached for the hand, thinking to help him up, but it pulled away from her reach.

"My f-father?" The tremulous voice sounded weak. "What...how...?"

Leonore stepped aside so that she was not blocking the torchlight, and its illumination fell on a pale face. Bleary, unfocused eyes gazed at her confusedly, and the acrid smell of an unwashed body wafted toward her, along with something else.

Fever. Leonore's heart sank as she dropped to her knees before the prince's prone form. She placed her hand on his face, easily fending off his feeble attempts to block her. "Be calm," she said, and Wesley's struggles subsided. His skin was alarmingly hot. "I am Leonore. Your father has sent me to get you out of here. Can you stand?"

"I...I do not think so." The feverish eyes were beginning to take on signs of recognition. "You say...my father sent you?"

"Yes, and Geoffrey and Wilfred and some others as well. They are waiting for us outside the castle." Dismay flooded Leonore as she watched Wesley struggle to sit up. She had not anticipated he would be unable to leave the castle under his own power. Even lying down, she could see he was a tall youth—how could he be otherwise with Liam as a father?—and she doubted she would be able to bear his weight.

With Leonore's help, Wesley was able to sit and lean against the wall. "I am sorry," he said, and even in his bedraggled state his apologetic grin was quick. "I am afraid I may not be of much help." He panted slightly—speaking was obviously costing him some effort. "What of the guards?"

"They have been disabled." The loud cry of a sexual climax belied Leonore's words, and she saw alarm on Wesley's face. "Do not fear, they are asleep. That was no doubt the sound of a dream. But they will not be asleep for long, and I must get you out of here."

Leonore tried to calculate how long it had been since she had cast the first spell. The interruption in the kitchen had slowed her down, and she feared she had only minutes before the men in the stables awakened from their happy dreams and started wondering about what had happened. She looked at Wesley again, gauging his weight. He was not so heavily built as his father. Perhaps she could carry him, after all.

Leonore thought about the many times she had seen peasant men and women lift seemingly impossible loads, and tried to remember the mechanics of how they had done so. She eyed Wesley speculatively. "Can you stand if you are able to lean against the wall?"

"I can try."

Leonore registered and approved of the determination in the prince's tone. "I will help you," she replied, getting to her feet. "Give me one hand and brace the other against the wall. We will do this together." After some maneuvering, Wesley faced Leonore with one hand against the wall to his side, and she levered him to his feet. He collapsed against the wall, but remained upright, trembling.

"Now, I am going to try to lift you." Leonore saw his eyebrows go up in surprise, but he nodded his understanding. The effort to rise to his feet seemed to have taken all his strength, and he did not protest as she lifted one of his arms and leaned forward with her shoulder toward him. "Now, just bend forward over my back."

Wesley did as instructed, and Leonore felt his weight shift away from the wall and onto her shoulders. Taking a deep breath and keeping one hand on the wall for balance, she straightened her legs and lifted him completely from the floor.

She staggered a little in surprise at the weight. He may not have been a heavily built man, but he had reached his full height and had inherited his father's broad shoulders. Leonore was not sure she could walk at all, never mind make it up a flight of stairs, but there seemed little choice but to try. Slowly, she turned and took a step toward the door. A small one. Her knees and back held, and she took another one, and another. She glanced at the torch, but both hands were occupied with steadying Wesley's weight. Oh, well, there were other torches in the main guard chamber and she should be able to see well enough.

The sleeping guard sprawled across the hallway was another problem. Leonore was making progress with her slow, shuffling steps, but she would have to step over the form. She debated whether to step over his legs—spread apart, so that would mean two barriers—or his torso, which was rather wider than she thought she could manage. At that moment, the man stirred in his sleep and twisted, bringing his knees together. Quickly, she stepped over the legs, and had to steady herself on the wall to avoid dropping her precious burden.

"Are you still with me, Wesley?" she asked.

"Yes," came the breathy response from somewhere behind her. "But I may have to...I may be sick."

Wonderful, thought Leonore, but she trudged grimly forward. She wished she could use a glamour to give her the strength that went with the illusion of physical size, but it was indeed a trick of the mind, and she was coming to the grim realization that she could not possibly carry Wesley out of the castle. She was barely making it across level ground, and the stairs would be beyond her capability.

As she arrived at the opening to the guard chamber, now strewn with twitching, moaning bodies, a sound drew her to a sharp stop. Leonore heard footsteps, and they were coming from the top of the stairs on the other side of the room.

"Where is everyone?" asked a bleary voice from above.

Damn. Someone has already awakened. Leonore's eyes darted around in panic. The doorway across the chamber led to the sleeping room, and there had been no other exit to the hall from which she had just carried Wesley. Her eyes were drawn to the other opening, which seemed more crudely hewn than the others and showed no flicker of torchlight.

There were tunnels leading off in all directions. Wilfred's words came back to Leonore as she began to pick her way between the unconscious guards. What else had he said? *Mellinor may have let them fall into ruin.* Ah, well, she had no other real choice. She had used all of her sleeping powder and could hardly concentrate well enough to manage a glamour while burdened with a barely conscious man who was threatening to vomit all over her at any moment.

"Hello?" The footsteps were coming tentatively down the stairs, and Leonore was afraid the voice's owner would clear the doorway before she could slip into the dark passageway. "Is anyone here?"

Panting with exertion, Leonore struggled the last few steps to the threshold of the passageway. She could only see a few steps inside, and what she saw was not reassuring. A tumble of broken stones and bricks indicated that some part of the ceiling had come down in the not-too-distant past. The floor was uneven and broken, and she was afraid there were more barriers hidden from the light. Still, it was her destination, and she stumbled into it just as she heard her would-be discoverer make it down the last few steps, to where he would be able to see the interior of the chamber.

"Gods, she has been here as well!" exclaimed the unseen visitor. "Wake up! You have been enchanted! Wake up." Soft thuds were heard, which Leonore assumed to be the sound of feet meeting flesh as the panicked man from the stable tried to awaken the guards. Groans erupted, but the spell had not yet worn off enough for Leonore to be worried that he would be successful.

"Pig shit." Leonore listened as the man ran back up the stairs. "Hallo, everyone down here! Help me wake the men!"

Leonore almost swore herself as she realized she had no chance of escaping up the stairs. She peered deeper into the passage, seeing more fallen stone. In the dim light cast by the torches in the chamber, it appeared the entire ceiling had come down, making an impenetrable barrier. She and Wesley were trapped!

But no—as her eyes adjusted to the dim passage, Leonore realized the wall of stones did not stretch completely across the tunnel's width. There was a hole, and it looked big enough to crawl through.

But not while carrying a full-grown man on one's back, she realized grimly as she stumbled closer to the opening. Reaching the tumble of stones that spread down from the hole, Leonore stopped, panting from exertion. She could hear the dim sounds of voices raised in alarm as the man from the stable succeeded in getting the attention of the others who had apparently awakened as well. Soon, they would return to the guard chamber, and she needed to be out of sight before they realized Wesley was no longer in his cell.

"Wesley, I have to put you down." There was no response. "Wesley! Wake up! I have to put you down!" She was answered by a groan, which she hoped meant he had understood her. In any case, she bent her knees until she saw Wesley's dangling feet touch the stone floor, and felt the weight that was making her muscles scream lessen ever so slightly. Inch by inch, she moved her body so the bulk of his weight was shifted from her back to her shoulders, until she was able to turn swiftly and catch him in an embrace. As he struggled to support himself, she eased him gently back on the fall of stones.

"Wesley! Can you understand me?" she hissed sharply into his face, and watched Wesley's eyelids flicker as he fought unconsciousness. He seemed to be trying to focus on her, but she could not really tell in the gloom. "We are going to have to crawl through that hole. I cannot carry you. I will try to help as much as I can, but you are going to have to do it mostly by yourself. Do you hear me?" Relief flooded through her as she saw him nod.

"Look at the hole. Look at it!" she said sharply as his head began to loll back. He seemed to stiffen his spine, and his head turned to look where Leonore was indicating. "Do you see it?"

"Yes," came his slow response. "I see it. Where does it go?"

"Out of here," was her terse response. "Start crawling." Voices seemed to again be coming from the top of the stairs. "NOW!" hissed Leonore, as she started to push Wesley up the pile of stones toward the opening. Luckily, it was not far. She barely felt the sharpness of the stones under her hands and knees as she forced the trembling prince up toward the opening. Silently, she sent a prayer to the goddess that the opening did not lead to a dead end.

Leonore looked up to see Wesley was only halfway through the opening. The voices behind her were definitely on the stairs, and it sounded like the group from the stable had been joined by those from the kitchen as well. "Hurry!" she whispered. "They're right behind us." She heard Wesley gasp as he took a tortured breath, then saw his muscles strain as he pulled himself the rest of the way through. Leonore scrambled through behind him, landing on top of him on a cold, rocky floor.

"Shhhh!" she said, afraid that the grunt of pain he had made when she fell on him would be heard, but the voices echoing in the outer chamber as the newcomers attempted to wake the groggy guards drowned it out. It was much darker behind the rock fall, but some light still filtered through the opening above their heads. Leonore pulled herself off Wesley then helped him into a sitting position. She squinted away from the light and toward the passage beyond, trying to make out any barriers. She could see none, but felt no movement of air.

A loud clamor from the chamber signaled that someone had finally thought to look in Wesley's cell and had discovered the prisoner's absence. Leonore strained to make out some sense from the shouts.

"She's taken the prince. To the gates!" said one voice. Leonore felt a sense of relief. Of course they would think they had already left the castle—they had no way of knowing she had only just managed to get Wesley out of the cell a few moments before they began to awaken. They would be looking for them above, not below.

Leonore was reassured by the sounds of arms being taken up and feet on the stairs when a great voice bellowed, "WAIT!" and all the other clamor ceased. As Leonore held her breath, the deep voice continued. "Look at the ground, here. Someone has gone in through here."

Leonore's heart sank. Of course, the dust and dirt had been undisturbed on the floor of the obviously unused passage. It had been, that is, until she had shuffled and struggled across the floor with a heavy burden, no doubt leaving a track that a half-blind man could follow in the dark.

"But the ceiling's all fallen down in there," argued another voice. "Do you think they could get through?"

"Oh, aye," said another voice. "There's a big gap still. See?" With growing alarm, Leonore saw the light coming through the hole brighten considerably, presumably because someone was shining a torch into the passageway. Looking up, the increased illumination allowed her to see why the hole existed in the first place—the timber that braced the roof had lost its support on one side only. The other support, cracked and more than half pushed out of its place, still barely held the remains of the cross timber. The loose stones above it had settled into a balanced puzzle. Leonore shivered at how precarious it looked. If she or Wesley had bumped it hard when they were crawling through the hole, the entire thing may have come down on their heads.

Leonore was suddenly on her feet. "Wesley, CRAWL!" she shouted, not bothering to keep her voice down. They would know she was here in a second. "Away from me, toward the tunnel. Go! Now!" Amazingly, Wesley started to crab away from the wall as he perceived Leonore's plan. Seeing him go, she launched herself at the crumbling support.

The moment her shoulder came in contact with the ancient timber, a dry *crack* sounded and the stones began to shift. Knowing she had only seconds, Leonore dropped away and rolled backward, away from the rain of dust, debris and huge stones that began pelting down as the cross timber gave way. Scrambling to right herself, she crawled away on hands and knees, catching up with Wesley as the rumbling of the falling stones drowned out the startled voices on the other side of the fall.

Darkness fell, black as velvet. Leonore and Wesley collapsed, coughing from the dust that billowed and engulfed them, the last bit of light winking away and leaving them in what Leonore sincerely hoped would not become their tomb.

Chapter Eleven

ဢ

Leonore lay on the floor and waited for her heartbeat to return to normal. She could hear the ragged sounds of Wesley's breathing as he struggled and coughed. She crawled to him, and groped to check his body for injuries. She found none, but his fever seemed higher than ever, his skin feeling as if he would burst into flames.

"That was...amazing," he gasped out between breaths. "I never thought a woman could...could..." Racking coughs cut off the rest of Wesley's comments.

"Save your strength," Leonore admonished. "It will not take them long to get through those stones." Already she could hear the sounds of voices, although very dim now, as they no doubt began the job of removing her temporary roadblock. As she assessed their situation, Leonore realized she could hear another sound as well. "Wesley, do you hear that?"

"Hear what?" was the faint reply.

"Running water." As Leonore had intended, Wesley held his breath for a few moments as he strained to listen.

Yes! It was definitely water.

"I...am not sure," said Wesley in a faltering voice.

"I am!" said Leonore. "Come on, the tunnel must lead that way."

"I do not...I cannot..." Wesley's voice was becoming ever more faint. Leonore was filled with pity. Here he was, in the grips of a fever that should be tended in a soft, warm bed with cooling cloths and drafts of herbs. Instead, he was crawling through a damp tunnel on the run for his life.

"Rest a moment." Leonore stood up slowly, feeling the walls around her. The ceiling here was much lower, and she had to duck her head to avoid scraping it. She would never be able to walk with Wesley on her back in the confines of this chamber. She was encouraged, however, at the barely discernable feel of a breeze on her face. The tunnel was clear ahead, even if she could see nothing. And now that she knew what to listen for, the sound of running water was unmistakable.

Keeping her hand on the damp wall, Leonore lowered herself back down to Wesley's side. "I cannot carry you in here, Wesley. Can you crawl?"

"Don't...think so." Wesley's breathing sounded worse, and Leonore felt a stab of fear. *Why was I so confident? What if I cannot save him?* It was the first time she had considered she might fail to save the prince. Surely, she would have had a premonition if...

There was the sound of falling rock and the dim voices on the other side of the obstruction temporarily grew in volume as they cursed. Apparently, the barrier was proving to be more difficult than the men had anticipated. *That does not mean they will not get through it eventually,* though Leonore grimly. She considered her options.

"Wesley?" She groped for his hand and found it, squeezing it lightly. "Can you hear me?"

"Yes." The response was faint.

"I am going to put you on my back again. I am going to try to crawl with you on top of me. But my hands will not be free, so you will have to hold on. Can you do that?"

"I will...try."

The maneuver turned out to be more difficult than Leonore had imagined, but after an interminable struggle, she found herself on her hands and knees with Wesley pressed against her back. His arms were around her chest and clasped above her breasts, and she could feel the heat of his fever through the cloth of her dress.

"Here we go." She began to crawl. Wesley started to lose his grip and cried out feebly, scrabbling ineffectively with his hands against her breasts, which already threatened to break free of her torn bodice. Leonore stopped moving, and Wesley regained his hold. She started forward again, moving more slowly this time.

"I...am sorry..." Between gasps, Wesley seemed to be trying to apologize. Leonore did not know if it was for inadvertently grabbing her breasts or for nearly falling off.

"Do not try to talk, Wesley," she said, beginning to breathe heavily. "Just concentrate on holding on."

Inch by inch, the two moved away from the rock fall in the pitch-black tunnel. Leonore knew her knees were scraped and bleeding, and her hands were taking punishment as well. Whenever Wesley started to fall, she stopped and steadied her weight on one hand as she grasped his with the other. And the sounds of men's voices and scraping rocks behind them never ceased.

"Ow!" Leonore gasped as both her head and Wesley's hit something solid. "Are you all right?"

"Yes," replied Wesley, probably untruthfully. Balancing carefully, Leonore lifted one hand and felt a solid wall in front of her. The sound of the water, suddenly much louder, was on her right. She had come to a sharp turn in the tunnel, and had crawled straight into a wall. She turned toward the sound and resumed her snail's progress.

"Steady now, Wesley," she said. "We are almost there." This was, she knew, ridiculous. She had no idea where they were. She had meant they were almost to the source of the running water, but there was no reason to believe they would be any closer to escaping or in any less danger when they reached it.

The tunnel seemed to slope downward, and Leonore realized from the echoes of her own progress that the tunnel was wider and the ceiling must be higher than before the turn. She stopped.

"Wesley, I am going to put you down for a moment so I can feel the walls here."

"Don't...leave me," was the barely audible response.

"I will not." She eased him from her back and helped him lean against a wall. "No, Wesley, you need to sit up." He had started to slide down to the floor, and she was afraid if she let him lie down, she would not be able to get him up again. "Just sit here with your back against the stones for a moment. Can you do that?" She felt him nod, and held her hand against his shoulder for a moment before standing.

Leonore stood tentatively, afraid of banging her head, but realized she need not have worried. She could not feel the ceiling, even when she reached high. Her hand found a sconce to hold a torch at about the level of her head, and she wished desperately she had one to burn.

To burn! Leonore almost banged her head against the wall in exasperation. She needed no tinder and flint to start a fire, only something that would burn once lit. The bringing of fire was one of the first spells she had learned, more years ago than she cared to count. She could find something to burn—a piece of her skirt, perhaps, and then...

And then what? They would be able to see, but only as long as they remained with the fire. They could not carry it with them, and its only purpose would be to make a warm place to sit while they waited to be captured. Leonore yearned to be out of this suffocating darkness, but not badly enough to waste whatever fuel was available for a few minutes of light. Not yet, anyway.

Leonore was jerked abruptly from her thoughts by the sounds of voices—many voices—in the tunnel. She knew instantly what had happened. The men had made an opening in the fall, and sound was no longer impeded by the rock barrier. Within moments, they would have a hole big enough to crawl through. Even though it had seemed like she had crawled a long way with Wesley on her back, Leonore knew it would only take the men a few minutes to cover the same ground.

"On your knees, Wesley. I need you to get up." She groped for Wesley's hands and began vainly trying to pull him out of his slumped position.

"I cannot—" he began, but she cut him off.

"You have to. They will be here in moments." She felt him pull one of the hands away and would have grasped it again, but she realized he was using it to brace himself against the wall. She used the other hand to lever him up, then leaned over and threw herself against him, just in time for him to collapse across her shoulder again. This time, she knew better how to steady herself with the weight but had less time in which to do so. She staggered a few steps in the direction of the water, hoping against hope she would not run into another wall.

The loud sounds of their breathing and her scraping steps echoed in the tunnel, then the timbre changed. Leonore felt the movement of air and realized they had come out of the tunnel into a larger space. The sound of rushing water was loud here. She took a few steps but stopped when cold water ran into her shoe.

She backed up. The voices coming from the tunnel sounded closer. The men must have broken through. They would be here in moments.

"Sorry, Wesley," she said as she bent over and deposited him on the floor. He groaned but did not protest. She grasped her skirt in both hands and yanked. There was a satisfying tearing sound as the skirt separated from the bodice along the seam. She kept tearing until it came away in her hands, then stepped out of it, dropping it on what she hoped was a dry place in the floor. She was already saying the words.

"*Censum...aduro...flagratio...exsucito...flammo...ignesco...in cendium!*" With a *whoosh*, the fabric burst into flame. Leonore squinted to protect her eyes from the sudden light and saw Wesley wince and turn his face away. The voices were closer now.

She scanned the chamber. It was smaller than she had thought, and the only way in or out seemed to be the passageway through which they had just entered. The floor of the room was more than half covered by a dark pool of water. Rivulets of water ran from the chamber's ceiling and into the pool, making the tinkling music she had followed.

A voice rang out, alarmingly close. Leonore's mind whirled. *Should I make a stand? I'll summon a glamour and...* No, that would not work. She could not keep that many men in thrall at the same time, and she'd never be able to get past them, never mind get Wesley away. If only there was another way out.

Leonore glanced again at the pool, which was anything but still with the many little spills and trickles falling into it. She was lucky she had not stepped into a sunken chamber with Wesley on her back and —

Realization hit Leonore like a thunderbolt. The ground where she stood and where her skirt was now beginning to burn out was bone dry. Even though water was running into it, the pool *stayed at the same level.* That meant the water running into it must also exit somewhere. *The tunnel was not the only way out of this chamber.*

"I see light ahead!" The voice was so close it could be no more than a few paces down the tunnel. Leonore had mere seconds to decide what to do, and she did it.

"Come on, Wesley, we are going for a swim." She grabbed Wesley under both arms and hauled him up with a strength she had not known she possessed. He struggled feebly against her, but panic and momentum conspired to make his attempts futile, and she half dragged, half carried him into the pool until she was waist deep in the cold water.

Immediately, she felt the strong tug of a current as the water tried to pull her toward the dim reaches of the narrow end of the chamber. With the water supporting Wesley's weight, she stepped farther away from the stone floor just as the embers that were once her dress started to flicker out and the glow of torches began to fill the gaping hole to the tunnel. She lifted her feet from the sandy bottom of the pool and let the current take her.

"What—" Wesley choked as water entered his mouth, and Leonore adjusted her position so his face was lifted from the water as she scissored farther from the edge. Torch light burst into the room and the dark shapes of men began to spill from the passage.

"Where are they?"

"What is this?"

"Something is burning here." The voices were a confused jumble as shouts echoed and bounced from the walls of the cave.

"There!" came a voice, and Leonore could just make out a figure pointing at them in the gloom. The current became stronger and swifter, and Leonore lifted her head to see the rock wall rushing toward them more quickly than she had anticipated.

"Hold your breath, Your Highness." Leonore just had time to take a breath and close her own mouth before the tug of the water pulled her, Wesley still held firmly in one of her arms, out of the dimly lit cave and into a black, spinning torrent.

* * * * *

The night was clear and the moon, though still not yet full, made deep shadows under the trees along the banks of the small brook. Leonore pulled Wesley's limp body up a shallow groove between tree roots and onto level ground. She collapsed next to him, their faces almost touching. Was he dead? How would she tell Liam she had failed him? How would she tell Geoffrey?

She reached over to touch his face, and was relieved to feel warmth. Even after soaking in the cool water, his fever still burned. But fever meant life, and she saw his ribs move slightly as he struggled to breathe.

I must make a fire. At least here I have plenty to burn. It was a good thing, too. What little was left of her clothing—the ragged remains of her bodice and the bottom of her short shift—were soaking wet and plastered against her body. Wesley's clothes were the same. She turned him over onto his back and pulled his arms around so he was in a more comfortable position.

She could see his features clearly in the moonlight. He was a beautiful young man. The fever must have come upon him in the last day or so, as no flesh had yet wasted from his well-muscled frame. She could see his father in his features, but Wesley's were more delicate. He was reputed to look a great deal like his mother, who had died when he was still a child. It must have been from her that he had inherited that golden hair and porcelain skin.

But Leonore had no time to consider this, nor to rest herself as she rose to her feet and began to search for fuel for her fire. She needed to get Wesley warm, and then to look for herbs to treat his fever. She winced as she felt a sharp pain as she got to her feet, noticing her foot was scraped and bleeding. It had probably happened during their wild ride through the underground watercourse that had led to this river.

Luckily, almost the entire trip had been in chambers where there was plenty of breathing room between the surface of the rushing water and the ceilings of the tunnels above, but on several occasions they had been sucked through smaller openings, as when they exited the first chamber. With no light, they had little warning and Leonore had taken in what felt like a lung full of water. She knew Wesley had fared even worse, and had been terribly afraid he would drown.

She hoped the underground stream and its aboveground counterpart had carried her far enough away from Mellinor's fort that his men would not soon arrive in search of her—or of Wesley, who was their true quarry. She had some concern that a fire might be seen, but she had little choice. She had to keep Wesley warm or he would be dead before morning.

Within a few minutes she had enough fuel to last for a short while, and she took it back to where she had left Wesley and again spoke the words that brought fire. This time, she made the flames smaller and added a small enchantment to assist in hiding the light from hostile eyes, although she knew this last would only work on a limited basis, and if the pursuers were not too close.

She went to Wesley, intending to make him more comfortable while she went in search of the herbs she would need to fight his fever. She dropped to her knees, ignoring the pain that radiated from her battered limbs.

"Wesley?" she asked. There was no answer. His face, which had looked peaceful a few minutes before, now was contorted and rigid. A frisson of alarm ran through Leonore. "Your Highness?" Wesley shivered, and Leonore could see his teeth were clenched.

With a cry of alarm, Leonore dropped to her knees and pulled his head and shoulders into her lap. Her hands roved over his face, chest and groin, and she uttered words of divining—words that would bring magic to tell her what happened in those parts of his body she could not see.

"Oh, Wesley," she breathed. "Oh my poor, dear prince." She felt the fever racing through his body as if it was in her own, felt his lungs fight to pull in air, felt his heart labor to beat. She felt his confused thoughts brush against her own as he wandered in the fevered hallucinations of the dying.

Dying! There was no time to look for herbs, no time to cajole his organs and his blood to fight the demons of the fever. Medicines could not heal him in time. Only magic could do it, and it would have to be the strongest magic Leonore knew.

There was no time. Leonore tore open Wesley's shirt and laid her face against his bare chest. His fever burned her cheek as she felt his shudders increase in intensity. "*Alito...confirnum...exsurgo...*" Leonore spoke the words of strengthening, but felt no difference in the war Wesley's body was waging—and losing—against the storm that wracked him. She sat up and tore off her bodice, pulling the shift apart with it. She would channel her own strength directly into him. She pressed her bare body against his.

"*Confirnum...invalesco...sanguen...alito...*" Leonore gasped out the words and heard Wesley moan. There was a slight giving way as his body began to accept the barest trickle of what she was trying to drive into him like a flood. Not enough. Not nearly enough. "Faster, it must go in faster," she gasped, as she tried to press herself closer. More contact, they needed more contact.

She pulled at Wesley's braies and they came away easily, the laces having already come undone in the ride down the river. She sat up and yanked his braies down to his knees. "*Vallo...invalesco... exsurgo...alito...*"

Leonore pressed her naked body full length against Wesley's, touching every inch of skin she could manage as she continued to chant. He moaned again, and she felt a more of the barriers between them drop and she pushed her strength and vitality into him. His heart labored and his lungs grasped vainly for more air. It was working, but too slowly. The fever was winning.

"*No!*" Leonore shouted aloud, addressing the sickness as if it were a living, breathing thing that could hear her and she could defy. "You cannot have him! I will not let you!" She entwined her arms and legs more firmly around Wesley's, pitting her will and her magic against the slippery, coiling force of the fever. "*Alito...exsurgo...*" She moved her skin against his, chanting in rhythm with the motion as she concentrated all her energies on the still-rising fever. "*...roboris... invalesco...*"

She felt the sickness peak, expand and then—waver. The surface of the fever seemed to develop cracks like a spider's web, and she forced tendrils of magic into the tiny openings.

"*Exsurgo...vallo...*" Leonore vaguely registered Wesley's growing erection, and shifted her body so as to let it spring free. She knew she could not let it find the home it was seeking—the evil illness might force its way into *her* body as she pushed it out of Wesley. Her breath was becoming uneven as she began to ride the wave of magic.

Wesley's moans became rhythmic and his hands grasped the air before him. Leonore could feel his lungs begin to pull air more freely, his heart beat more surely as his moans turned to incoherent shouts.

"*Confirnum...roboris...*" Leonore's chant went on and the very leaves and trees seemed to take it up and she continued to press herself against him, no longer feeling anything but the power. "*Alito...exsurgo...*"

Wesley heaved and would have thrown himself from the ground had Leonore still not held him fast. She felt a sudden warmth and wetness as his seed shot against her hip, and his dry skin was bathed in the sweat of a breaking fever. He screamed then his body relaxed. His body grew limp, but Leonore could feel it was the relaxation of sleep, not fever, and let the lassitude that engulfed him like a flood take her down with him.

Chapter Twelve

ഔ

"My lady?"

Leonore stretched luxuriantly, awakening from a dream she could not remember but knew was lovely —

"Ouch!" Leonore sat up abruptly, her movement having caused her to rub her buttocks against a sharp rock. She blinked, and found herself looking into Wesley's face. He was sitting up, leaning toward her with his weight supported by one arm. The remains of his torn shirt still hung about his shoulders, but his braies had been pulled back up.

But it was his face that drew Leonore's attention. Wesley looked startled, but did not draw back as she put her hand to his cheek, now rosy and clear. There was no sign of fever. He smiled, and Leonore realized it was in response to her own expression. She laughed.

"Wesley, you are well, and I am delighted."

"Yes, my lady, I am well." The cheeks became even rosier, and Leonore saw he was blushing. "Are you," his eyes ran down her body then returned abruptly to her face, "well also?" His blushed deepened, and Leonore glanced down to see what had embarrassed him so. She laughed again. She was fully naked, and grass and dirt clung artfully to her skin in various places. Her nipples were rosy and erect—must have been the dream—and Wesley stared at them as if he had never seen a naked woman before, which she knew he'd almost certainly had.

"I am a bit sore and stiff from our adventures," she said, tentatively stretching each limb in turn and wincing as various bruises and cuts made themselves known, "but I think a rinse in the river will take care of most of the damage." She got to her feet and raised her arms over her head.

She saw Wesley gazing at her as if at something not quite real. "I will just be a moment," she said, and she moved down the banks of the stream and into the water. It was fairly shallow, and she had to get onto her knees to wash the dirt from her face and hair. She ran her hands along her arms and legs, luxuriating in the feeling of fresh water as it tingled against the few scrapes and bruises she encountered. It would be lovely to relax in the cool water and rest—

Geoffrey. The thought came crashing down on her like a cold rain shower, and she abruptly rose from the stream and hurried back to where Wesley still sat as if uncertain what to do next.

"My shift," she said, looking around for the remains of her garment. "Have you seen it?"

"Your shift? No, I—"

"Ah, there it is." She picked up the forlorn garment. "Not as bad as I feared," she said, putting it on. She shivered against its dampness and looked up to see Wesley staring at her breasts, easily seen through the damp garment. "You might give me your shirt."

"My...yes, of course, my shirt." Still blushing, Wesley stripped off the remains of his shirt and handed it to Leonore. Though torn, it was large and could be tied together in the front, and hung down far enough to mask where Leonore's ruddy pubic hair was easily discernible. She searched for the remains of her bodice, hoping it could be somehow used to make her more presentable, but it turned out to be a mere shred.

"Does my bottom show through the shift? She turned her back toward Wesley and waited for an answer. It was not immediately forthcoming.

"Well?" She turned toward him. "Does it show?"

"Er...yes." He said. "But I will not look if you do not wish it," he added hastily.

"It is not you I am worried about," she said. "It is Sir Geoffrey and his men."

"Geoffrey?" Wesley's brows rose. "Is he near?"

"Not near enough," said Leonore. "I am to bring you to him before midday, or he will attack the fort in order to rescue you by force. And he does not know it, but he is both outnumbered and, most likely, expected."

Wesley gaped. "Do you know how to find him? I mean, do you know where we are?"

"Not precisely," said Leonore. "But I think the river flowed away from the fort toward the east, and the rendezvous point is to the north of the fort. We should be on the opposite side of the road from him. So, if we travel northwest until we reach the road, I should be able to find him."

"But, my lady..." Wesley started to protest, but stammered to a stop.

"What is it?" asked Leonore impatiently. "We shall have to hurry."

"It is just that I do not...I cannot..." Wesley struggled to regain his composure, then started again. "I do not remember everything that happened last night, and I must ask...I need to know..."

Leonore hid her smile. He really was very young, even if no longer a child. "No, Wesley, we did not make love. But I had to lay my body against yours, skin to skin. It was part of a strength spell I was casting in order to...well, I do not have time to explain it all right now, but you did not dream it."

"I know that I did not dream it. But I thought I might have...that we might have..." He grinned shyly at Leonore. "What I cannot really remember is your name."

Leonore laughed aloud. "My name? Oh, Wesley!" She laughed again. "I am Leonore, and I should probably stop calling you Wesley and address you as 'Your Highness' as is appropriate for a subject of your father's realm." She bowed politely, aware what a comical sight she must make with her wet hair and odd garb.

"Well met, then, Lady Leonore," said Wesley. "I suppose we should hurry and find Sir Geoffrey." He grinned again. "Unless you know somewhere we could find some food."

Yes, a very young man after all. "I am afraid not, Your Highness. Geoffrey's men will probably have something in their packs, but until then we must move with all speed."

* * * * *

Wesley turned out to be a good woodsman, probably due to his love of hunting, and the bright day cast shadows that made gauging their direction quite easy. Nevertheless, Leonore feared any delay would have disastrous results, and urged him to maintain a speed that made conversation difficult.

Once they found the road, however, speech was possible. Leonore expected questions from Wesley, but found the young man uncharacteristically pensive.

I really should have a word with him before we encounter Geoffrey. The thought had come unbidden, but Leonore was annoyed with herself. She realized she did not want Wesley to blurt out something Geoffrey would misinterpret. *Why should it matter? I was saving his life!* And yet Leonore knew it would indeed matter to Geoffrey, and felt cross with herself that she cared.

Sighing, she turned to Wesley, even though she had no idea what she was going to say to him. She was surprised by the beatific grin he wore. "What is it Wes—Your Highness? You seem very pleased with yourself."

"I have figured it out," replied the prince in a smug tone. "It all makes perfect sense to me now."

"What have you figured out?" Leonore was baffled.

"Why my father sent you to rescue me instead of Geoffrey and the soldiers."

Ah, so that is it. Leonore was curious whether Wesley understood the political subtlety of foiling Mellinor's plot without a show of military force. It appeared the young man had a good grasp of the skills that would eventually serve him as king. She decided to let him show off a little. "Please explain, Your Highness."

"He wants me to marry you."

"WHAT?" Leonore stopped dead in her tracks.

Wesley's grin became, if possible, even wider. "It is so very obvious, once I thought of it. Father has been after me for months to find a suitable bride. I admit, I have been dragging my feet, and lately he has become annoyed."

Wesley, seemingly oblivious to Leonore's shock, kept walking as he voiced his astonishing theory. Realizing she was standing as still as a statue with her mouth agape, Leonore closed her lips and hurried to keep up with the tall youth who, blissfully ignorant of his audience's reaction, continued to warm to the theme.

"He said I would start siring bastards among the castle servants, and I needed to get married before I created complications I would later regret." Wesley chuckled, apparently at the memory of the argument with his father. "But I told him the suitable women he kept inviting to the castle—along with their toadying fathers—were, well, *boring*." He turned to smile sweetly at Leonore.

"So he found someone he knew I could never be bored with," he continued. "*And* someone magical. Father is very interested in magic, you know. This way, he can have me safely married off to a woman who is both exciting and obviously a lady, and gets a true magician in the family all at the same time." As Leonore mentally stammered for something—anything—to interrupt this astonishing fantasy, he went on.

"Who knows, he might even have magical *grandchildren*. How he would *love* that!"

At this last outrageous statement, Leonore felt a well of hysterical laughter begin to bubble up through her chest. Squelching it with tremendous effort, she finally managed to unfreeze her tongue. "Oh, Wesley! I think you may have misinter—"

"YOUR HIGHNESS!" A shout from the ridge above them stopped both Leonore and Wesley in their tracks. Looking up, they saw Wilfred, his gleaming smile framed by his red beard, hurrying down the slope toward them. "And Lady Leonore! Well met, well met indeed."

* * * * *

Geoffrey's relief was palpable. He was, of course, happy to see Wesley—he had always been fond of the young prince and his wellbeing was the very reason for this journey. But it was the sight of Leonore coming over the ridge that had loosened the invisible cords that had increasingly bound his chest as the night faded into morning and the sun had moved toward its midday zenith. He had not realized how frightened he had been for her welfare until the relief struck him. He was glad all the men's focus was on the pair, as his knees had actually weakened for a brief moment, before he strode forward with the rest. He was glad he had the presence of mind to approach the prince first, as was correct for a knight in the king's service.

"Your Highness!" Geoffrey reached Wesley and clapped him on the shoulder, then pulled the grinning young man into an embrace. He then held Wesley at arm's length, scrutinizing him for signs of his captivity. "You look hale and hearty. You must not have been kept locked in an underground chamber for weeks on end after all." He looked over Wesley's shoulder at Leonore and gave her what he intended as a wry look. Apparently, her supposed vision had not been as accurate as they had thought.

But the look Leonore gave him in response was not what he expected. He had thought she would make some gesture to gracefully concede he had been right and she wrong. Instead, she looked — flustered.

"But I *was* underground, Geoffrey. For what seemed like forever." Wesley gently extricated himself from the knight's grasp and stood back so he could tell his tale to a wider audience. "It was cold and damp and full of rats. And I was not hale and hearty — I was near death, to hear the guards talk." He shuddered visibly at the memory, and Geoffrey saw his own wonder mirrored on the faces of the other knights.

"What happened, Your Highness?" Horace asked eagerly, and the group began to take on the arrangement of a storyteller surrounded by spectators. A flash of movement caught Geoffrey's eye, and he turned to find Leonore at his elbow.

"I do not wish to interrupt," she said, obviously wishing to do precisely that, "but perhaps we could don some more appropriate garments and get something to eat before we continue?" Horace's face turned toward Leonore, and his blush showed it was the first time he had noticed her near nakedness.

Geoffrey could see the outline of Leonore's legs though her shift, and realized she was carefully keeping her back to the group. If she stepped forward the soft, rounded curves of her buttocks would no doubt be clearly visible. The thought caused a familiar tightening in his groin, and he hastened to agree with her suggestion.

"Yes, of course," he said. "Wilfred, I believe we still have some foodstuffs, poor as they may be. Horace, you are probably closest to His Highness in stature — will you not search your pack for something suitable? And I believe I may have a cloak that will suit the Lady Leonore. My lady?" Geoffrey gestured, indicating Leonore should precede him. He was pleased he had contrived both a moment to be alone with her and an opportunity to walk behind her and enjoy the view.

Again, Leonore's reaction was not what he expected. She gazed after Wesley, her eyes narrowed, and looked as if she would call out. Obviously frustrated as the prince disappeared with Horace and Morgun, she pursed her lips and turned to face Geoffrey, who was still gesturing for her to walk ahead.

"Oh, all right," she snapped, and marched in the direction indicated.

Geoffrey was annoyed. Did she not *want* to be alone with him? Their last moments together had been of passion. *Not quite the last*, he corrected himself. He winced internally as he remembered the feel of his fist connecting with the soft flesh of her lip and the *squish* as the delicate skin broke under its force. He had not wanted to do it, but she had insisted. Surely she could bear him no ill will for the injury?

The memory of her bleeding lip brought him up short. "Leonore," he said, and something in his tone must have reached her, because she turned to face him.

"Yes, Geoffrey? What is it?"

"Your lip. It is," Geoffrey brushed his knuckles lightly against her mouth, "perfect. I was sure it would still be bruised."

"Oh, that." She probed with her own fingers. "The healing spell must have reflected back from Wesley and taken care of my injuries as well."

"Healing spell? Is that why he looks so well?'

"Yes." Leonore turned and took the last few steps to where Geoffrey's cloak lay folded next to his open pack, ready to be returned to his mount. She picked it up, but he took it out of her hands and settled it around her shoulders.

"So, you healed him before escaping the castle?" Geoffrey asked, wondering why this conversation felt so awkward.

"Not exactly." Leonore had her eyes on her breasts, where Geoffrey's hands were fastening the cloak's intricate ties. "Geoffrey, I need to speak with you about the…the magic I used to heal Wesley. I did not have time to heal him in the fort.

The sleeping spell I used on the guards was starting to wear off and—"

"Sir Geoffrey!" Horace's voice came from close behind them. "Begging your pardon, sir, but Wesley, I mean His Highness, refuses to continue with his tale until you return."

"We will be right there, Horace," said Geoffrey, "but His Highness is going to have to tell his story quickly, because we need to get mounted and on our way before someone comes looking for us."

"They probably are already," said Leonore, "although if they are following the river, they will be looking in the wrong direction, at least for a little while."

"The river?" asked Geoffrey. It might explain Leonore's odd attire.

"Yes, I was about to tell you. Geoffrey was too ill to walk, so we had to—"

"Excuse me, Lady Leonore, but Prince Wesley is waiting." Again, Horace interrupted.

"Yes, Leonore, let us allow His Highness to tell the tale. He seems very eager to do so."

"So it would seem."

Leonore sounded cross. Geoffrey was puzzled with her obvious irritation. Why not let the boy have his moment of glory? "Come, Leonore, we will have ample opportunity to talk on our way back to the castle. We will have to camp tonight in any case." Geoffrey gave her what he hoped was a significant look. Could she not see the implications of a night spent in the wood? They would steal away together, and—

"Sir Geoffrey?" Horace was practically jumping up and down.

"Come Leonore." Geoffrey held out his arm. Leonore sighed as if in resignation and took it.

"All right." Leonore's face took on an inscrutable expression as they returned to the remains of the fire, where

Wesley was eating a hard biscuit and drinking from a wineskin.

"Ah, Geoffrey, you are here. And Lady Leonore may have to help me with the story, as for parts of it I was too ill to be completely sensible." He looked eagerly at Leonore, who nodded. She was still wearing that odd expression, Geoffrey noted.

"You probably all know the night they took me," Wesley began, looking around for the nods of the others. "It was the middle of the night and I was sound asleep. Two or three men grabbed me up and blew some kind of smoke into my face, and I think I passed out." He winced at the memory. "When I woke up, I was in a stone cell, and felt as if I had drunk a barrel of brandy the night before."

"Did you know where you were?" Wilfred asked.

Wesley shook his head. "Not at first. But eventually I heard Mellinor's name mentioned, and knew I must be at the Baron's old fort." He looked grim. "It was the darkness that was the worst. Sometimes I could see a little torchlight coming under the door, but except for when someone would bring me food or drink…" He trailed off.

Geoffrey picked up the story. "You have been gone almost three weeks, Wesley. It must have seemed very long."

Wesley's eyebrows rose. "Was it as long as that? I never thought to ask Leonore." He looked at her and, if Geoffrey was not mistaken, blushed. "I mean, I knew it was a long time, but once the fever took hold of me, I really had no sense of days passing. It was all just a blur."

"Fever?" Horace looked at Morgun, and both men looked nervous.

"Yes, but I am quite well now. No need to fear." He smiled at Leonore. "The Lady Leonore cured me." This time Geoffrey thought he caught something significant in Wesley's glance, but Leonore did not react.

"I am not sure how long I was ill. I kept getting weaker and weaker, and it seemed I slept all the time. The guards would come in and give me water and try to get me to eat, and I knew I should try, but it became more and more difficult." Now deep in his memories, Wesley's tone became almost hollow.

"By some of their comments, I could tell they thought I was going to die. They were worried Mellinor would be angry, because he needed me alive in order to bargain with my father." The prince gulped, and for a moment he looked younger than his twenty-one years. "I knew I did not want to die, but somehow I could not make myself really care. I even thought it would serve Mellinor right if his plot fell through because he kept me in that horrible hole."

Wesley's voice shook, and Geoffrey almost moved forward to take his arm, but in that way the very young have of changing in an instant, a sunny smile broke out on Wesley's face.

"Then the most amazing thing happened. I was lying as I had for days—too sick to know whether I was awake or asleep—when I was visited by an angel." Triumphantly, Wesley held out a hand toward Leonore, as if indicating she should take over the story. When she did not, he shrugged and continued.

"I thought at first I had died and was in heaven, but," Wesley grinned ruefully, "not only did this particular angel *not* comfort me, she kept insisting I had to stand up. I knew a *real* angel would never be so cruel." The prince smiled appealingly at Leonore, apparently trying to engage her in his humorous account, but she seemed unwilling to participate.

"The next thing I knew, she was dragging me out of the cell and we were climbing over the guards, who were sleeping all over the floor. I remember being carried, I think…" His brow furrowed, and he appealed to Leonore. "Lady Leonore, you are going to have to explain what happened next. I really do not remember."

Leonore's reluctance puzzled Geoffrey, but he saw her straighten her shoulders and take a deep breath, as if the task was inevitable and she was prepared to make a good showing at all costs. She told the tale simply—the awakening guards, Wesley's inability to walk on his own and her decision to drag the nearly dead prince into the underground pool, hoping its currents would carry them from the dungeons.

"When the current had carried us as far as it would, I climbed out onto the river bank. I was able to start a fire." Leonore's voice faltered, as if she was reluctant to continue. She glanced at Wesley, but she had apparently not yet reached the part of the story he remembered. Looking resigned, she went on.

"His highness was…well, the river had saved us from capture, but it had not helped his condition. I was afraid he would die. So, I used magic to heal him."

"What kind of magic?" asked Wilfred. This question seemed to send a jolt through Wesley, who hurried to Leonore's side.

"Very powerful magic," he said, blushing crimson. "It was quite amazing. Hard to describe. Very…mystical." Wesley took Leonore's hand, which seemed to surprise her, but she did not resist.

"After the spell, I fell asleep. We both did. We were exhausted." Wesley seemed agitated, and the easy demeanor he had shown when he started the story had vanished. Geoffrey felt suspicion begin to rise through his body with a discernible heat. *Just what kind of magic is he talking about?*

"We woke up early, and had to dress ourselves as you saw. Our clothes were mostly destroyed during the…the time in the river. Leonore knew what direction we needed to take." Wesley gave Leonore a look of…what? *Pride?* Geoffrey saw that the prince still grasped Leonore's unresisting hand, and had moved to stand very close to her.

"So we started here. And that was when I realized…"

Leonore opened her mouth as if to interrupt the young man, but it was like trying to stop the flow of a river once the damn had burst.

"That was when I figured out why father had sent Leonore to rescue me. It is the king's intention that Leonore and I be *married*!"

Chapter Thirteen

જી

Geoffrey felt the blood rising to his face even as it drained from Leonore's. *Healed him, did you? I am quite sure I know the exact manner in which you healed him.* He saw Leonore's mouth fly open as if to speak then watched her eyes flash between Wesley and himself. He knew the look on his face probably did not invite explanation, and he fought his fury like a beast.

Leonore must have realized the futility of saying anything, because she closed her mouth and, for a moment, her eyes. She stood next to Wesley, who was still clutching her hand, and remained silent as Horace, Morgun and even Wilfred peppered the couple with questions.

The couple? Was this what Leonore had wanted all along? A royal marriage? Geoffrey felt like the village idiot.

Wilfred turned from Wesley and said, "Sir Geoffrey, is this not the most surprising news? I would never have guessed—" Geoffrey's visage must have stopped him. Frowning, he went on. "What is wrong, Geoffrey? Are we in danger?" The old knight's hand went to his sword.

Geoffrey took a deep breath and willed his voice to be normal. "No, but we will be if we do not get back to the castle before some minion of Mellinor's arrives there with a message that Wesley has been rescued. The king very much wants to deliver that particular news himself."

Wilfred nodded and turned. "Horace, Morgun, you will have to hold your questions for now. We must return to the castle with all speed. Wesley, we have your horse."

With reluctance, the younger knights obeyed the command and soon the troop was mounted and on the road. As the swiftest rider, Horace was sent ahead to warn the castle guard to intercept anyone arriving with a message for Mellinor.

Geoffrey's own horse was skittish, and he knew it was probably because the beast could sense his own unease. His rage threatened constantly to overflow, and as he rode at the front of the column, he could feel Wilfred's keen and curious eyes on him. He could hear Wesley's laugh behind him and imagined Leonore smiling at her new conquest, but he refused to turn his head to look at the happy couple. He ground his teeth.

A movement on his right caught his eye. To his dismay, he saw Wilfred had dropped back to allow Wesley to draw up next to him.

"So, Sir Geoffrey," said the glowing young prince, "you have not said what you think of my news."

Geoffrey resisted an urge to punch the king's son. "It is...most surprising, Your Highness."

Wesley laughed. "Yes, I think you could safely say that. I was just telling Father the other day I was not ready to choose a bride. Little did I know the wily old devil had a plan to change my mind." Wesley chattered on happily, but Geoffrey ceased to listen, only grunting occasionally when a pause in the monologue seemed to require his response.

Scheming bitch! Geoffrey could now see clearly how he had been used. First, Leonore had seduced him to fuel her damned magic. Then, at the first opportunity, she had jumped into bed with the king.

Righteous anger welled in his chest, feeling oddly satisfying. He had let her talk him into forgiving her once already. His hands still held splinters from their rut in the wood above the fort. He felt his face burn with mortification at how easily she had convinced him of her blamelessness.

"Geoffrey?" He realized Wesley must have asked him a question, and he had failed to respond.

"Forgive me, Your Highness. I was thinking about…what lies ahead."

"But that is what I was asking you about. Do you know what my father plans to do to Mellinor?"

"No." Geoffrey's answer was curt, even to his own ears. He looked at the prince's open, guileless face and sighed. It was not Wesley's fault. How could such a young man be any match for a woman as beautiful and perilous as Leonore? He softened his tone before continuing.

"I believe that whatever he does, it will be a private matter. He does not want his other guests to know of the plot, and he will probably find some way to turn it to his political advantage. My plan is to take you straight to him, and to do so without being seen."

"If anyone can make this into a triumph, it is the king," agreed Wesley. "And now, if you will excuse me, I must return to Lady Leonore. We have a lot to talk about, you know."

Before Geoffrey could respond, the prince had dropped back and Wilfred was moving to regain his place. *I should probably warn the young fool*, he considered, then thought better of it. He decided it would make better sense to speak to Liam. Surely the king would not fall so easily under Leonore's spell.

Unless he already has. With this unhappy thought, Geoffrey urged his horse to a slight increase in speed, as the afternoon wore much too slowly toward evening.

* * * * *

"I would have words with you."

Geoffrey looked up from the remains of his dinner, startled. He had not heard Leonore come up behind him. *Damned witch is quieter than a fox.*

"Will your *betrothed* not miss you?" Geoffrey did not try to hide the venom in his tone.

"He is not my betrothed," said Leonore evenly. "And in any case he has gone with Morgun to hunt something for breakfast."

"So you have come to tell me how it was not your fault that your *healing* required you to play the whore with the Crown Prince? Within a day of doing the same with his father?" There was enough moonlight that he could see Leonore's wince, and he felt a measure of satisfaction.

Leonore bristled. "Is that what you think I was doing? Playing the whore?"

"It is not a difficult conclusion to reach, Leonore."

"Indeed!" Leonore was breathing audibly. "I did not ask to speak to you so you could...you could *abuse* me."

"Abuse *you*?" Geoffrey was incredulous. "After you have used me as your...your..." He struggled for the right word. He could not think of anything bad enough, so he abandoned the thought and went on.

"And now you have no less than a king's son in your thrall. Was that your plan all along, Leonore? A royal marriage?"

"You know perfectly well I have no intention of marrying Wesley. He is just confused."

Geoffrey snorted. "I dare say. He has no experience dealing with witches."

"That is not precisely true," said Leonore.

Geoffrey could see she was angry, but still under control. Like he had been all day. Well, he was tired of holding in his rage. He wanted to let it out like a great fireball of heat. But more than that, he wanted to see Leonore lose that damned composure she seemed to always wear, except when she was in the throes of sexual satisfaction.

"Do not even try to imply Wesley carries any blame in this matter, Leonore. I know well how difficult you are to resist when bent on seduction."

"I did not seduce Wesley!" She was trembling now.

"Oh, and I suppose he seduced you?" Geoffrey laughed at the ridiculousness of this idea, and knew the laugh was far from pleasant. "You found his charms irresistible and swooned in his arms." He was baiting her, and was far from ready to stop.

"I did *not* succumb to his charms. I used my magic and—"

"Ah, yes, the magic. A convenient excuse, Leonore, and becoming all too familiar." Geoffrey did not remember standing up, but found himself standing nearly nose to nose with Leonore, whose eyes flashed a green that could be seen even in the dim moonlight. *She is almost ready to explode. Good.*

"Were you running out of strength, Leonore? Did you need a little more fuel for your fire? You could not wait to get back to me, so you found the most convenient source and filled yourself up on it!"

"He was DYING, Geoffrey! DYING!" Leonore's voice finally lost its restraints and she shouted—no, shrieked her response. "I could feel the life leaving his body. He had minutes to live...seconds! I had to save him, and what I did was the only way."

"So, as usual, you had no choice!" Geoffrey thundered right back at her.

"None! If I had not shoved as much power into him as quickly as I could, he would be dead now, Geoffrey. Would you prefer I had let him die?" She was panting like a bellows, rage seething from every pore. Geoffrey drank it in and wanted more.

"Do not try to turn this around on me, Leonore. I never wanted you to go into that dungeon after him in the first place. I could have come in with my men, and—"

"And lost who knows how many of them! There were forty armed men in that fort, Geoffrey. Even if they had not killed you, you still would have found Wesley too weak to make it back to Liam."

"So you say."

Leonore's voice turned to a hiss and her eyes narrowed. "Do you accuse me of *lying*, Geoffrey?"

"You? Lie?" Geoffrey let the sarcasm drip from his words. "A *lady* like you? Never!"

"I never claimed to be a lady, Geoffrey."

"It is well you did not!"

"What is that supposed to mean?" Leonore said through her teeth.

"It means you are about as far from a lady as it is possible to be. You are both a whore and a witch, and you have fooled me for the last time."

* * * * *

Leonore did not remember ever being so angry. Her heart pounded in her ears and her very skin crackled with rage. *How dare he? How dare that sanctimonious, self-righteous...* Even in her thoughts, words failed her.

Leonore forced herself to still and breathe deeply. She had been stomping through the wood away from the camp with no thought other than to put as much distance between Geoffrey and herself as possible. She had been afraid she would lose control and summon forth the most malevolent spell she knew and put that arrogant whoreson bastard in his place!

Breathe. Just breathe. Leonore looked around for a place to sit and saw a large rock that would do. She knew eventually she would have to return to the camp, before the hunting party returned and Wesley came looking for her.

She winced at the thought of the prince. She had not wanted to make him look like a fool in front of the knights, and there had been no opportunity to speak with him privately and correct his misunderstanding.

How could he have come to such an outrageous conclusion? It made sense the king would want Wesley to marry soon, and avoid getting into some unwanted entanglement. Leonore wondered if Liam knew Wesley had lain with Chellasandre. She had known, of course, as soon as Chellasandre had described the failed attempt at creating a power circle and divining Wesley's whereabouts. That was what Leonore had been about to tell Geoffrey when he had accused her of being a liar and a whore.

Leonore felt the pounding of her heart start to speed up again, and returned her concentration to calming herself. She could not afford to expend any energy on anger. Although she never would have admitted it to Geoffrey, at least not now, she was almost completely depleted.

Whereas sexual gratification had always been the source of her power, the act of healing Wesley had transferred strength to him, not the other way around. Coming so soon after the multiple spells she had employed during the rescue, and the plain physical exhaustion of carrying Wesley and fighting to stay afloat in the river, the spell had drained Leonore almost dry.

A small laugh escaped Leonore. Just moments ago, she had been telling herself she had stomped away from Geoffrey to prevent herself from hurting him. *I could not cast a spell on a newborn right now.*

So why had she run away? For run Leonore had, even if under the pretense of righteous indignation.

Be honest with yourself, Leonore. What are you really feeling? Why are you so angry?

Because I care what he believes of me, came the answer. And finally Leonore's shoulders slumped and her heartbeat steadied. She knew she had touched the exact center of the truth, and it was not a truth that brought her comfort.

Men had called Leonore a whore in the past. The very nature of her magic and the narrow-minded beliefs of the majority of men made this inevitable. Leonore had gotten over being stung by the opinions of others long ago, and had shrugged off insults as easily as water ran from a duck's back.

But Geoffrey was different. The moment Wesley had blurted out his ridiculous assertion, she knew she had been secretly hoping to keep her manner of healing the prince a secret from the noble knight. She had wanted to resume their budding relationship and learn more about him, and to reveal more about herself to him. But all had come crashing down when Wesley unwittingly revealed what she had done. Actually, what she had *not* done. She had not actually coupled with Wesley, nor touched him in any way that was sexual, but the healing had been sensual and arousing, as was all her magic to some degree.

Leonore did not feel shame — not precisely, anyway. After all, she had done nothing to be ashamed of. She had used her magic, and it had saved Wesley's life. It had been the right thing to do — the only thing to do. And yet...

"Leonore?" A voice called from the direction of the camp, and Leonore knew she had a task to perform. She had to make Wesley understand he had made a mistake in assuming she would be his bride. She was not especially worried about hurting his feelings. The prince had not known her long enough to truly be in love, and young men recover quickly.

Leonore sighed. *If only the same could be said for Geoffrey.*

Chapter Fourteen

ත

"I will come back when His Majesty is ready to see you." The servant girl bowed her way out the door and left Leonore in the quiet room. It was comfortable enough, but she longed for her bed and her bathing pool, not necessarily in that order. She smelled like horse and campfire smoke, and was stiff from sleeping on the ground. Until she regained enough strength for a self-renewal spell, she would have to settle for the everyday cures of sleep and hot water.

They had arrived at the castle just before the time of the midday meal, which had been fortuitous. It created the perfect venue for King Liam to bring Wesley out and seat him in front of all his guests, with no explanation other than a recent return from a hunting trip. Geoffrey, Wilfred and the rest of the knights in the party had rushed to the dining hall to take their seats. Wilfred said he did not want to miss Mellinor's reaction when the prince walked in, to which Geoffrey had wryly replied, "I will just go along in case his reaction is to head straight for his horse."

Leonore had declined the King's invitation to sit at his table and watch the proceedings, pleading fatigue. She was sure Geoffrey thought she was lying about being tired, which was fine with her. She had been careful not to reveal how weak she was feeling, and was almost certain she had fooled Geoffrey.

She lay on the small bed — little more than a pallet, really — and smiled as she remembered the conversation with Wesley the night before.

"How can you be sure my father does not wish you to marry me, Leonore?" the Prince had asked. "I think I know his tactics better than you do. I have studied them all my life."

"It is true I have known the king but a short time," Leonore replied with complete honesty. "But I was party to the discussion when he decided to send me to Mellinor's fort to rescue you. I am quite sure he sent me only because using my magic rather than force suited his ends."

"But you have no idea how he cares about magic, Leonore." Wesley was not yet prepared to give up his argument. "He is *obsessed* with it."

"I am quite aware of King Liam's interest in magic."

"Then you know how pleased he would be to have a person of true power in his household."

Leonore sighed. She knew Wesley was excited by the idea of taking a witch as a bride, and also of having a lusty woman in his bed. He was obviously besotted with her, but his argument lacked the true passion of love.

"What I mean to say, Wesley, is your father knows I would not be suitable as a royal bride."

"Why not? You are obviously a lady." Wesley's words reminded Leonore of Geoffrey's recent assertion of the precise opposite point of view, and made her smile rather painfully.

"Well, among other things, I am too old."

"That is ridiculous. I mean, I know you are older than I am, but not by more than five or six years, I am certain."

Leonore smiled. "It is very kind of you to say so, Wesley. But I fear my appearance may be somewhat deceiving. My magic has the effect of reducing some of the more unpleasant ravages of time." Leonore had never thought of this as anything but a benefit, but occasional misunderstandings occurred, and this was one of them. "I am a great deal older than you may think. Too old to have children, I fear."

"Surely not!" Wesley was aghast at the notion.

"It is true. And you are the heir to the throne. You must take a wife who can bring you children. So even if you are right about your father's wishes…" Leonore let the sentence trail off, and watched as understanding and resignation spread over Wesley's features.

"I see." He took Leonore's hand and looked at her soulfully. "You are right, Leonore. Although I can imagine no bride as…as enticing as you, we cannot be married." He continued to gaze at her, and Leonore realized he was trying to break this news to her gently. She stifled a smile and struggled to keep her expression serious. The best she could manage was neutral.

"Of course, you could always be my mistress." Wesley looked hopeful, but Leonore shook her head.

"No, Wesley, I do not think that would be appropriate. I am not the sort of woman to be happy hiding in the background, and my presence would prevent you from finding a bride who will make both you and your father happy."

Wesley had ultimately agreed to this argument, with only a minor attempt at reluctance, and she had told him he must clear up the misunderstanding with the knights. Leonore had watched Geoffrey surreptitiously to see his reaction to the prince's announcement, but his face had revealed nothing. Normally she would have been able to sense his emotions, but even the little energy required to divine such things was more than she could afford to expend right now.

This reminded Leonore of a much more immediate problem. The events of the past several days had caused her level of magical reserves to fall far lower than she had allowed for many years. There was a simple and direct way to replenish them, of course. But she could not imagine herself lying with anyone but Geoffrey, and he was hardly speaking to her at the moment.

But I can still imagine it. The idea should have occurred to her sooner. Leonore had seldom indulged in sexual fantasies, at least not for any longer than it took to find a likely subject and play them out. Yet she knew that any sexual pleasure, even if it was self-administered, could bring her *some* power, small as it may be. At least enough to keep her going until she could get home and arrange for a new helper. Dunfred had already fulfilled his agreement and belonged to Cortlyn now, but surely there would be other young men in the village who were preparing for marriage and would benefit from her instruction.

But she did not want to think about some faceless, nameless young man just now. She wanted to think of Geoffrey. *Geoffrey.* She had seen his naked body only by moon and candlelight, whereas by day he had been covered from foot to neck and wrist, and sometimes even clad in light armor and mail. Now, she would take a moment to imagine stripping him of each item of clothing in the full sunlight of…of a forest glade with a running stream and a lily-covered pool. Yes, that was perfect.

As physical exhaustion and the simple comfort of the clean bed pulled Leonore into sleep, she began to dream.

* * * * *

The light made sparkling jewels on the surface of the water and glinted on the gems on the hilt of Geoffrey's sword. So too sparkled the jewels on Leonore's hands, as she reached out to unbuckle the belt and scabbard.

"Usually my squire does this for me."

"I shall be your squire today, Sir Knight." After gently laying the sword aside, she moved to the short corselet of mail that protected his chest. She was surprised to find him naked beneath it.

"Where is your tunic? Will not the rings hurt your flesh?"

"Does it not please you to see me thus?" Geoffrey's tone was teasing, and Leonore realized the links were too few and too light to stop a spear point. The thought he had worn such a garment for her enjoyment made her smile.

He got down on his knees before her so she could pull the mail shirt over his head. The moment his arms were clear, he wrapped them around her body and pressed his lips between her breasts. Leonore realized she was naked, too. When had she removed her clothes?

Geoffrey spun her around in his strong arms and grasped her buttocks. "And will I take you as a man takes a squire, then?"

Leonore was surprised. "Have you taken a man thus?"

"No, but I have never seen a man whose bottom was like two perfect orbs of alabaster. Feel what the sight of it does to me, Leonore." Without releasing her, he got to his feet and pushed his shaft into the cleft that divided her posterior. She felt it pressing against a place not yet ready to receive it, and shifted her weight. It slid between her legs, its head brushing between her wet labia and catching against the bud of flesh that guarded their joining. Hot liquid gushed from her body and slicked his member.

Shuddering, he turned her to face him then lifted her from her feet. Weightless, she wrapped her legs around him. He held her so the tip of his shaft was touching her wet, pulsing lips, then slowly lowered her weight until she was impaled on his jewel-hard flesh. She spasmed involuntarily, squeezing and tightening as he lifted her slowly up and down. His flesh felt hotter than that of a fevered man, sliding in and out of her body as she writhed and moaned.

"This is not," she panted, barely able to speak, "how a man takes a squire."

"But this is." Geoffrey lifted her free from his cock, which stood out from his belly. Then he gradually settled her weight again, rocking her slightly backwards and moving his hips so the head of his shaft rested against the tightly shut opening behind the still throbbing lips.

"It is so very hot!" she gasped, as she felt the barrier ease slightly open at the probing of his member, slick with her juices. It seemed impossible that it would fit into so tight a sheath, then her muscles suddenly relaxed and he slid partway into that unaccustomed opening.

There was a moment of pain – or something close to it, and then the deep, visceral sense of pleasure caused her to squeeze him so tightly that he gasped aloud. The tightening spasm was followed by another loosening of the passage, and she felt him slide yet deeper inside of her. They cried out in unison and he pulled back and plunged all the way into her until the flesh of their bodies met.

Such pleasure could not exist. Now they had joined completely, her body yielding easily and he withdrew and drove, withdrew and drove. Geoffrey lowered himself to his knees and laid Leonore's shoulders on the mossy ground, still holding her lower body and spread legs high in the air and never coming unconnected.

Climax after climax rushed through her and still he pounded on, each stroke bringing her as far as she thought possible, only to be exceeded by the next. His cock seemed to grow to an impossible size, filling her like a great, rutting horse as she bucked beneath him.

"Geoffrey, Geoffrey!" She said it like one of her magical chants, over and over as the rhythm pounded on. "Oh, Geoffrey!" The very leaves and trees seemed to take up her cries as he continued to pound himself against her. She could no longer feel anything but his amazing, supernatural bigness as his organ seemed to fill every inch of her body, threatening to split her asunder.

Panting now, Leonore felt his shaft begin to throb and contract, growing bigger and smaller as her body squeezed and contracted to match each surge. Suddenly, there was a huge expansion she thought might burst her apart and then she felt his seed blast into her as if pumped from a bellows. He screamed, and her voice rose to mingle with his, their feral howls rending the night air like a jagged blade.

* * * * *

Leonore felt she had barely dozed off when footsteps outside her door told her the servant girl was returning. Reluctantly, she stretched and smoothed her borrowed shift. She was surprised to see fresh garments had been brought while she slept. *I must have slept longer than I thought.* The servant was probably returning to help her dress.

"Has the king called for me?" she asked. "If you can just give me a moment to straighten my hair—"

"No, the king has not called." At the sound of the familiar, high-pitched voice, Leonore turned her head sharply.

"Chellasandre. What are you doing here?"

"I heard you were back." Chellasandre glided into the room and examined the clothes that had been laid out for Leonore, running a tiny hand along them. "And high in the king's favor, I see. This gown was made for the queen, before she died. I do not think she ever wore it."

The smaller woman held the tunic up in front of her body, and squinted to examine herself in the polished bronze mirror that hung on one wall. "Of course, she was a cow like you. I would be lost in such a garment. And this color does not become me." She dropped the garment on the floor and turned to examine the girdle critically.

"You do not seem to suffer from a lack of finery," said Leonore dryly. As on the previous occasion they had met, Chellasandre was dressed in a grand fashion, as if preparing for a ceremony. Her hair was elaborately dressed and her eyebrows had been shaved and repainted.

"I am a person of consequence in Liam's court. My appearance is important."

"You have not said what you are doing here, Chellasandre. I am in no mood to bandy words with you." Leonore picked up the garment Chellasandre had let fall, then took the girdle from her fingers.

"No? Well, I will not be staying long. I have just come to give you a little advice."

"Then give it and be gone." What was this tiresome woman up to? Leonore could feel a tiny spark of power within her, probably the remnants of the lovely dream, but did not want to waste any of it probing a mind she had already found to be distasteful.

"You think to displace me." When Leonore would have protested, Chellasandre cut her off. "Do not bother to lie to me, Leonore. It is obvious you have both King Liam and Sir Geoffrey in your thrall, and now probably Wesley as well." Chellasandre's voice lowered to a hiss.

"I have been here eleven years, Leonore. Eleven *years*. And you are here for mere hours, and suddenly everyone is talking about how you have *real* magic and King Liam sends you off on a task that should have been mine. *Mine!*" Chellasandre paced back and forth, reminding Leonore of nothing so much as an angry cat. "And then I hear that idiot Horace babbling to the kitchen maid that Wesley is on his way back to the castle with his new *betrothed*, the Lady Leonore, and—"

"We are not betrothed, Chellasandre."

"Yes, I know that," was the snapped reply. "Morgun came in and said it had all been some sort of misunderstanding. Not as smart as you thought you were, hmmm?"

"What are you talking about?"

"You thought you could take him away from me, did you not? Well, you were wrong." Triumph was plain in Chellasandre's voice.

Leonore laughed aloud. "You thought I wanted to take Wesley away from *you*? Oh, Chellasandre, wherever did you get the impression he was yours to begin with?"

The younger woman drew herself up with indignation. "Wesley and I have been…have been…"

"Yes, I know, you have been coupling with him. And so, I would imagine, have half the maidservants in the castle. He is twenty-one, Chellasandre. His cock gets hard when the wind blows. Yours was just a convenient hole in which to bury it."

"*Bitch!*" Chellasandre launched herself at Leonore, claws out. Leonore barely had time to drop the dress she was holding and catch the flailing wrists.

"Careful, Chellasandre. You have already had a taste of my power. Are you so eager to feel it again?"

The catlike features did not soften, but Leonore felt the muscles in the arms relax and saw the fingers lose their threatening arch. She was relieved—she might be able to summon enough power to defeat this woman, but it would be both a great waste and an arduous effort.

To Leonore's alarm, Chellasandre spoke words that nearly mirrored her own concerns. "Are you sure you can overcome me so easily, Leonore? You feel...different."

Leonore felt the brush of power as Chellasandre's mind probed her own. Quickly, she shielded herself, but she was not sure the strain of doing so did not show on her face. She did not trust herself to speak until she felt Chellasandre's efforts drop away, defeated for now.

"Do you really want to find out?" she bluffed. "The difference you are feeling is nothing more than plain fatigue. I have been rather busy the last few days, and would prefer to rest my powers, given the choice. But if you insist on making me rise to the occasion..." Leonore shrugged, as if it would be a simple matter to vanquish anything Chellasandre threw at her.

"Perhaps another time." The younger woman sauntered a little too casually toward the door.

"You never did give me that advice." Leonore was gratified to see Chellasandre's shoulders stiffen. She turned slowly.

"Do not try to turn King Liam against me, Leonore. You will have cause to regret it."

"I will consider what you have said," replied Leonore. "But King Liam makes his own decisions. I think he will come to know what you are all on his own, if he has not already done so."

Chellasandre looked as if she wanted to come up with a scathing response, but merely whirled and marched out. The door closed behind her with a rousing slam.

Leonore sagged with relief. She looked longingly at the bed, considering whether it was too late to resume her nap. Liam might be tied up for hours, dealing with Mellinor and celebrating the return of his son. On the other hand, he could call for her at any moment.

Another set of footsteps in the hall made Leonore's decision for her. She turned to face the maidservant, ready to ask for hot water. Her mouth opened to speak, but the words never came out.

Sir Geoffrey leaned casually against the doorframe, his expression unreadable.

* * * * *

By all the gods, she is beautiful. The thought came unbidden to Geoffrey. The late afternoon sun shone from the window and outlined her frame through the light shift, stirring memories of the pleasures of her body.

Geoffrey did not want to think about her charms right now. It made it difficult to hang on to his anger. To remind himself that he had every right to be angry with her. That she was a deceitful, grasping, arrogant—

"What is it, Geoffrey?" Leonore's tone was impatient.

"Am I interrupting something?" He sought to keep his tone free of menace, but was not certain he was succeeding.

"No, but you just missed Chellasandre."

This surprised Geoffrey, and for a moment he forgot his purpose in coming here. "What did she want?"

Leonore shrugged. "She claimed it was to give me a warning. Although I am not sure whether it was about turning the king against her or trying to steal Wesley."

"*Steal* Wesley? Do you mean to say she and Wesley—"

"Yes, apparently. Although I suspect she places more importance on the matter than he does."

Geoffrey stared at her for a moment, then threw back his head and laughed, startling himself. It felt good — really good. He had not realized how much tension he had been holding in his body and for how long. Suddenly free from the stiffness of anger, he sat down on the bed. Leonore looked at him like he had gone mad.

"I am sorry, Leonore," he said, wiping his eyes. "I was just thinking how Chellasandre must have imagined herself about to become a princess. What a shock it must have been to find out you had accomplished in a few hours what she had been trying to do for *years!*" He began laughing again, and watched a reluctant smile come to Leonore's features.

"I never really was betrothed to him, you know."

"So you say."

"Really, Geoffrey, you know I was not. It was just a wild notion of Wesley's." She frowned. "Although I can see now that it must have been Chellasandre who gave him the idea in the first place."

This was a new idea. "It was Chellasandre's idea that Wesley should marry *you*?"

"No, of course not." Leonore sat down next to him. "Wesley did say, however, that his father would be well pleased to have someone with my powers in the family, especially if I could supply him with magical grandchildren. I doubt he came up with that idea on his own."

"*Magical grandchildren?*" Again, the laughter rose up in Geoffrey, making him helpless to stop. "*MAGICAL GRANDCHILDREN?*" He rolled on the bed, quite beside himself.

"Geoffrey, stop. It is not that funny." Leonore's voice was stern, but her own mouth was twitching.

"I am sorry, Leonore, but I suddenly had a picture of you surrounded by a brood of tiny witches and wizards, spouting spells and turning one another into...into toads!"

Leonore was laughing now as well. "I assure you, Geoffrey, I have never turned anyone into a toad in my life!"

"Maybe you should," he hooted. "How about Chellasandre? And Wallix!" He doubled over. "Turn him into a big, pale, ugly toad."

"With a sonorous croak, like his voice." Leonore was getting into the spirit of the jest. "Cannot you just hear him saying" she attempted to croak like a frog, "'*Leono-o-ore and Geo-o-ofrey...I shall have my reve-e-enge*'."

"He had better say it quick," said Geoffrey, whose nose was starting to run. "The dogs will eat him in less than a minute. They *love* toads."

"Geoffrey, you must stop. I cannot breathe." Leonore sat up straight and made what looked like a valiant attempt to regain her composure. Geoffrey watched her from the pillows.

"I have been very angry with you, you know," he said, but his voice held no venom. "I have been calling you terrible names all day."

"And I with you." Leonore reached out and smoothed back the hair on Geoffrey's forehead. Her hand felt cool, and he resisted the urge to grab it and kiss her palm. Her expression grew serious.

"This thing with Wesley," she began then stopped, frowning. "I know you do not want to hear it, but I really did have not a choice."

Geoffrey thought about it. "I believe you used your magic out of necessity, Leonore. But I also think you enjoyed it."

She considered this carefully. "I do enjoy using my power. I always have, even when no sex is required. The coupling..." She took one of Geoffrey's hands in hers. "As it happens, I did not have to resort to that to heal Wesley. But I did lie against his naked body, skin to skin. I will not lie to you and say it was not pleasurable. But I would not have done it if there had been any alternative. And I drew no power from it."

"You did not?" Geoffrey looked at Leonore carefully. While still very beautiful, she did look tired. He could see faint lines around her eyes and a certain hollowness to her features. "No, I can see you did not."

"Coming so soon after all of the spells I had to perform during the rescue, I fear that healing Wesley took rather more out of me than I care to admit," she said. "But I was too angry with you to let you know."

"You could have just found someone else to…fuel your fire."

"I could have," she said, "and under other circumstances I would have done so. But I did not want to."

"Why not?" Geoffrey asked quietly, almost afraid of the answer. "What is different about these circumstances?"

Leonore sighed, and her hand stroked his. Geoffrey watched a shudder run down her body and felt one answer in his own.

"I did not want to be with anyone but you."

It was what Geoffrey had wanted to hear, but the pangs of jealousy were still very strong. "That is odd for you to say, so soon after practically making love to the Prince. And the King, for that matter."

"Yes." He had expected an angry reaction, but Leonore remained very quiet. "It is odder than you know. But it is quite true, nevertheless. Liam and Wesley were…well, they were necessary. Pleasurable, but necessary. But after each one I felt guilty, I suppose." She gave Geoffrey a direct look. "I have never felt guilty about using my magic before, Sir Knight. And I think it was not the magic that made me feel that way. It was the pleasure."

"What are you trying to say?"

She took a deep breath. "It did not feel right to take pleasure from anyone other than you. Not once I had known you."

Geoffrey was stunned. "Leonore, I—"

"My lady?" A voice from the doorway caused both their heads to turn. A maidservant stood there, carrying a ewer of water. "His Majesty is ready to see you now."

Chapter Fifteen

ഔ

King Liam was beaming. "Lady Leonore, I am your most humble servant." He grasped both of her hands in his, raising her from her deep curtsey. "I have had the most extraordinarily successful day, and it is all due to you. So you must not bow to me, at least not today, and not in the privacy of my chambers."

Leonore allowed herself to be waved toward a comfortable chair, and watched the king seat himself opposite. A servant poured two goblets of wine and departed at Liam's signal.

"I was sorry to miss the midday meal with your guests," said Leonore. "Did all go as you intended?"

Liam's smile widened. "Even better. Mellinor turned the color of milk, and would probably have fled had he not found Wilfred suddenly at his elbow." He chuckled at the memory. "He was delivering a message, well overheard, that Mellinor was to wait upon me after the meal. I do not think he enjoyed his meat very much today. Although he appeared to have made up for his loss of appetite with an exceptional thirst for the wine."

"And your meeting went as you had hoped?"

"I do not think I need trouble myself that Mellinor will oppose me in the future. Especially now that his entire family will remain in the castle, as my most honored guests, of course, until after the ceremony where we all swear fealty to the High King."

Leonore smiled, indicating her appreciation of Liam's skill at handling the situation. "And how did you find Wesley,

Your Majesty? You had little time to greet him before you had to take him directly into the meal."

"He left me only a few moments ago." The king put down his goblet and eyed Leonore directly. "He told me something rather surprising about you, you know. He says he asked you to marry him."

Leonore felt the color rise into her cheeks. "Yes, well, he...I believe he misunderstood your intentions."

Liam laughed heartily. "Yes, he gave me a rather sheepish account of how he 'figured out' my plan to get the two of you together. I gather you straightened out his misapprehension."

Leonore smiled, relieved. "Yes, Your Majesty. I told him it would not be appropriate."

"He said you told him you were too old to bear children. Which, I must admit, I find rather hard to believe."

"Well, perhaps my body would still be able to perform the task," Leonore admitted, "but I am well past the point where the idea of motherhood holds any appeal."

Liam was silent. Leonore regarded him over the rim of her goblet. *He is still a very handsome man.* But the mad desire she had felt on the night of the divining spell was gone. It had been, she realized, only an affect of the magic after all.

"Wesley was right about one thing, Leonore." The king stood and stepped before her. He held out both hands, and she put down her goblet to take them. He raised her to her feet. "It would be...I would be immensely pleased to have a person of power in my household."

Leonore looked into the kind eyes. "You have Wallix and Chellasandre."

Liam made a scoffing noise. "Magicians at best."

"No, my king. At least not Chellasandre. Her motives...well, I would watch her very carefully. But there is power there, if she but takes the time to learn to use it sensibly."

"And will you teach her, Leonore? I think not." Liam's gaze grew warm. "And to compare her power to yours is like balancing a candle against a wild forest blaze."

"What would you ask of me, Your Majesty?"

Liam smiled. "Right to the point, eh? Leonore, a man would never grow bored with you."

Leonore inclined her head in acknowledgement of the compliment, but continued to wait for an answer. The king sighed and went on.

"Actually, Leonore, the question is, what would you ask of me? What can I offer that will entice you to remain here?"

"You are the king. You could simply order it so."

Liam nodded. "I could. But I do not think it is an order that could be enforced, if you were not in accordance."

Leonore gently extricated her hands from the king's, and turned away. "I am your most loyal subject, and I will always come if you have need. Is that not enough?"

"No."

The abruptness of Liam's answer surprised Leonore, and she turned to face him. He went on, "That night in the tower, I felt magic. Real magic, Leonore. All my life…"

He began to pace the room. "When my brothers died, I thought I would have to give up my dreams and turn my mind to my responsibilities. And I have done so, Leonore. I have given all my attention to bringing peace and prosperity to the people who live within the borders of my lands."

He turned to her, and a light seemed to glint in his eyes. For a moment, she saw the pagan god she had screamed for on the night of the spell.

"And now I am given a chance to have both. To have my country *and* magic. To be king and sorcerer." He came to stand directly in front of her, and grasped both her shoulders. "And to have the most exciting woman I have ever known in my bed. Should I turn away from such a chance, Leonore? Would I ever forgive myself?"

Leonore searched Liam's face, and the pagan god faded to be replaced by a kindly king. She reached up and touched his brow.

"I gave you magic that night, Liam. And you gave it back to me. But it was the means to an end. It cannot be like that all the time. Not even for me." She stared into his eyes, willing him to understand.

He dropped his hands from her shoulders and began to pace again. He stopped short, and turned to face her.

"I am prepared to make you queen."

Leonore felt her jaw drop open momentarily. "Queen?"

"You have said you wish to have no children, and I already have my heir. With your help, we could prepare Wesley to be a king such as the land has never known." He stepped before her and, to her horror, dropped to his knees. "Marry me, Leonore."

Leonore felt as if the wind had been knocked from her lungs. *Two royal proposals in two days.* That would be a tale to tell, if there was ever anyone she would wish to tell it to! She looked down at Liam, on his knees before her.

Why should I not take this opportunity? As a queen, could I not use my power for the benefit of all?

This time, it was Leonore's turn to take the king's hands and raise him to his feet.

"Your Majesty…Liam." She searched his face. "Your offer is so very generous. But I cannot marry you." Liam opened his mouth as if to speak, and she placed a finger against his lips.

"You are about to swear fealty to the High King. It is said he plans to make his reign one of Christianity. While I believe there is a place for…for my kind of magic in a Christian kingdom, the king's priests may not agree. It is my intention to give them no reason to take notice of me."

Liam looked as if he were about to argue, but she went on. "You cannot show up at the High King's court with a wife who is well known to be a witch, Liam. It would force the High King to publicly confront the situation, and I believe that is a confrontation we would both prefer to avoid."

When Liam spoke, his voice was low. "You speak of the political reasons we cannot be married, Leonore."

"You are the king. Everything you do has political implications."

"True," he said. "But is there another reason you do not wish to be my wife, Leonore? Do you find the idea...distasteful?"

Leonore suppressed a smile. Even a king wants to be desired by women, she supposed. "No, Liam. You are a very attractive and virile man. Any woman would be pleased to share your bed."

"Any woman except you."

Leonore considered how best to answer this statement, but found the real reason coming from her lips, even as the realization dawned upon her. "I find that I love another."

The king looked surprised. *Little does he know how my own words have shocked me.*

Suddenly, Liam laughed.

"Well, my Lady Leonore, you have given me the one argument I cannot overcome." He took her hands again, but this time his look held affection rather than determination. "May I give you a kiss of congratulations?"

"You may."

Liam leaned forward and kissed her lips. His kiss lingered, but held no real heat. They drew back and gazed at one another for a long moment. "Thank you, Leonore."

"It has been my pleasure to be of service, Liam."

The king withdrew, and returned to his chair.

"May I ask the name of the lucky man?" he said lightly.

Leonore smiled ruefully. "I think, Your Majesty, that perhaps I should inform him first."

This time, Liam's laugh was relaxed and genuine. "Then I think you should take your leave and do so."

Leonore curtseyed. "With Your Majesty's permission, I intend to do just that."

* * * * *

Geoffrey simmered with rage. *Whore. And to think I had begun to believe her when she said she wished to be with no other man.*

When Leonore had been called to meet with the king, she had asked Geoffrey to wait for her so they could continue their conversation. He had imagined making love to her, helping her regain her strength even as they mended the angry words that had come between them.

But the waiting had grown long, and Geoffrey had become impatient. He had decided to go to the king's chambers and perhaps meet her coming out of her private audience.

He had been surprised to find no guard, and the door opened just a crack. Uncertain whether to wait or to go in, Geoffrey had listened for a moment to see whether Leonore had already left.

"I am prepared to make you queen." Liam's strong voice had come clearly from the slightly opened door, stopping Geoffrey in his tracks. He had stepped back in shock for a few moments then opened the door to see Liam drop to his knees at Leonore's feet and ask her to marry him.

"Your offer is so very generous..." Geoffrey had barely heard the beginning of Leonore's response before he had turned and fled down the corridor, nearly running over the returning door guard, who had probably gone to relieve himself.

Magical grandchildren! What had seemed so funny just a short while ago rang in his head like a taunt. No doubt Leonore had decided to sweeten the enticement. Why settle for magical grandchildren when the king could have a little witch or sorcerer of his very own?

Geoffrey stumbled from the foot of the stairs into the court. He looked around for a place to go to vent his rage, his eyes settling on the main entrance opposite. He hurried in that direction, only to find himself tripping over several of the ever-present dogs. He glanced around, realizing an unusual number of the huge animals were milling in the court. Why would they be here at this hour?

Puzzled, Geoffrey looked around more carefully, and saw a familiar form slip quickly around the corner into one of the archways. His eyes narrowed.

What is Wallix up to? He followed the man, intending to call out, when he heard a high-pitched voice raised in agitation. It was Chellasandre, and she seemed to be annoyed with Wallix. He paused, his back against the other side of the arch, and listened.

"We have to do it *now*, Wallix. I tell you, she has done something to drain herself of power. We must strike before she has the chance to build it up again." The woman sounded exasperated. "Do you not wish to be rid of her before she turns Liam against us and we find ourselves with no home?"

"Of course I wish to be rid of her," replied Wallix, his stage whisper a stark contrast to his usual melodious tones. "But you have never before done so strenuous a spell. And it has been many years since I myself—"

"Yes, yes, I know." Chellasandre soothed. "But I was practicing earlier and I am sure I can do it. And when I complete the binding spell, I can draw from both of our powers simultaneously. Now, let us go over the words of the chant one more time, without the blood to complete it. She could come down the stairs any moment. We should be watching."

"Is Geoffrey gone?" Geoffrey heard the shuffling of slippered feet against the stone floor on the other side of the arch, and he eased himself father back into the shadow of the wall. A pale hand appeared around the edge of the arch, and Geoffrey held his breath as Wallix peered toward the door at the other end of the hall.

"He is not out there now," was the whispered response to Chellasandre.

"Then we must keep our eyes on the foot of the stairs and be ready for Leonore. Come now—repeat the words with me while we wait." Barely discernible Latin phrases whispered from the other side of the arch.

Geoffrey remained where he was, wondering if he should interrupt this fascinating conversation. Obviously, the two planned to try to work some magic against Leonore. He could prevent them from doing so, of course. But he doubted the two charlatans had enough power between them to cause Leonore any trouble, even in her weakened state.

And she may have been faking that as well, he thought sourly. He was still undecided whether to intervene or to watch the two magicians make fools of themselves when the sound of footsteps on the stairs caught his attention. A sudden intake of breath and the instant cease of the chanting told him Wallix and Chellasandre had heard it as well.

"Oh, hallo!"

Geoffrey peered out of the darkness to see who Leonore was greeting, and saw her scratching the shaggy head of one of the larger dogs. Several of the other animals clustered near her, vying for attention. "What are all of you doggies doing in here tonight? All you great, big, lovely doggies!" Leonore was rubbing another dog's ears, and a third tried to press his head under her hand.

Suddenly, a *crack* like a great wooden beam breaking was heard and the court was filled with a weird light. The sound of the Latin chanting resumed, and Chellasandre and Wallix stepped from behind the arch.

Chellasandre's hands were upraised and her eyes seemed to glow a fiery red. She spoke in an eerie voice.

"*Canis auctorita...caedo...evito...interficio a Leonore.*"

The hands came down, and Geoffrey thought he saw a light streaming from them, but somehow it was a dark light, if such a thing was possible. Wallix stood behind Chellasandre with his eyes closed and the palms of his hands on either side of her head. The two chanted together, but Geoffrey could only hear one voice.

"*Canis...iuguolo...leto...turcedo...morsus...*"

As the stream of light leapt from Chellasandre's fingertips, Geoffrey saw his own horror reflected on Leonore's face. Without thought, he ran to throw his body between the source of the light and Leonore.

He saw the moment Leonore recognized him hurtling toward her, then saw her eyes look over his shoulder. Reaching her, he turned and thrust her behind him. He raised a hand, hoping to somehow fend off the stream of power that Chellasandre was casting their way.

To Geoffrey's astonishment, he saw the light was not directed toward Leonore at all. Instead, Chellasandre seemed to be focusing the magic on *the dogs*.

"*Auctorita latrator...neco...ictus...caedo a Leonore et Geoffrey!*"

At the sound of his own name in the chanted words, Geoffrey looked at Chellasandre's face and saw a weird glee. Her eyes seemed to crackle with power and hatred. Whatever she was trying to do to Leonore, she had decided to extend to him as well.

An odd keening arose, and Geoffrey thought that the very stones were answering Chellasandre's call, when he realized the sound was coming from the dogs. Their fur stood on end, and Geoffrey felt the hair on the back of his own neck rise at the sight. The keening gave way to growling, as a dozen pairs of canine eyes turned upon Geoffrey and Leonore.

"Geoffrey, she is telling them to kill us." Leonore's voice, coming from directly behind Geoffrey, was strangely calm. "I fear I do not have the strength to stop her."

"Get back, you curs!" Geoffrey stomped his foot and waived his hands in a shooing gesture. Liam's dogs had always obeyed him—had done from childhood—and he expected them to give way. But the growling rose in volume, and he had to pull his hand back to avoid snapping teeth.

"*Canis…turcedo…morsus a Leonore! Interficio a Geoffrey!*"

Several of the dogs crouched as if ready to spring. Geoffrey tried to keep himself between them and Leonore, and again he heard her voice in his ear over the unearthly growling.

"When I say 'go' Geoffrey, you must run for the door. I think I can push them back for just a moment, long enough for you to go for help."

Geoffrey shook his head frantically. "I will never get back in time, Leonore. They will tear you to pieces."

"They will tear us *both* to pieces if you do not heed me! Do as I say, Geoffrey. Now *GO!*" She gave him a little shove.

Geoffrey felt a sudden gust of hot wind blow past him from behind and one of the biggest dogs, caught in the very act of springing, fell backward as if pushed. The others cowered, and Geoffrey heard the chanting falter for a moment before it resumed.

"*CANIS   AUCTORITA…CAEDO…EVITO…INTERFICIO A LEONORE!*" screeched the Chellasandre-Wallix voice.

"Run Geoffrey, NOW! You only have seconds!" Leonore's voice urged him on, and Geoffrey ran a few steps then stopped and turned.

The dogs were inching forward on their bellies toward Leonore, and Geoffrey found himself running back toward her. Reaching her, he pulled her into his arms. She was stiff, as if still holding on desperately to the last of the power she could summon.

"You will...die with me," she gasped. "You must...save yourself."

"LETO...NECO...ICTUS...MORSUS..."

"I cannot abandon you Leonore. If we cannot both flee, then we will die together."

Chapter Sixteen

✂

Leonore felt the last of her power fading as the chant rang on and on in her head. *Who would have ever thought I would be defeated by Chellasandre? At least I was able to save Geoffrey.*

But, no, Geoffrey had come back and taken her in his arms. Was this a dream? Leonore struggled to hold the frayed ends of the power that barely restrained the snarling, snapping dogs. She could feel their hot breath on her skin and in a moment one of them would overcome her feeble magic and spring.

I must convince Geoffrey to run. His arms were around her, but if she let go of her power enough to argue with him, the dogs would be upon them. Drawing every vestige of strength she had left, Leonore reached into the empty well of her magic and found...

Power! Leonore found power rising and swelling in her like a spring bubbling up through frozen ground and breaking free through the crust of ice that covered it. It ran up through her center, through the core of her womanhood and out to her limbs. She could feel her hair rising and coiling, and for a moment caught a glimpse of Geoffrey's astonished face as he reacted to the light that was spilling all around her.

The chanting stopped and Chellasandre screamed. Wallix dropped his hands and backed away from Chellasandre, who fell to the floor and began to writhe, holding her hands to her temples and shrieking even more loudly. The dogs cowered and whined.

The sound of running footsteps sounded on the stairs, and the king's guard burst into the court, followed closely by Liam himself.

"What is going on here?" Liam bellowed then stopped as he came to face Leonore. "My lady, why are you filled with magic? And what have you done to Chellasandre and Wallix?"

Wallix was on his knees, holding his hands to his head in a mirror of Chellasandre, who still writhed and moaned, although her shrieks had become less ear-splitting.

Before Leonore could answer, Geoffrey spoke. "Chellasandre and Wallix tried to kill her, Liam. To kill us both. Leonore..." Geoffrey stammered, unsure himself what Leonore had done.

"I stopped them, Your Majesty." Leonore breathed deeply, willing the glowing power to subside but having little success. She had never felt so powerful, not even after the most potent rite, and was not sure how to contain such pure, bubbling ecstasy. "Forgive me, but I think I will need a few moments to return to myself." She almost giggled at the gaping stare of Liam's guard, who stood as if frozen in the thrall of a glamour.

But what Leonore was experiencing felt nothing like a glamour. That was something that she pulled around herself like a cloak. This felt more like a fountain pouring forth from within, from her very center. Her body pulsed as with sexual pleasure, as if she had just had the most fulfilling sex of her life.

Judging by the looks of wonder on both Geoffrey and Liam's faces, she looked as unusual as she felt. With great effort, she pulled back the power and settled it into herself with a final tingle and throb. The light in the room faded back to dim torchlight, and Geoffrey's face showed relief. Chellasandre's moans had turned to quiet sobs.

"Get them out of here," said Liam. "Throw them in the oubliette. The guard sprang to do as ordered. Wallix obeyed dumbly as the guard directed him to help the quivering Chellasandre to her feet, and the three marched away, leaving Leonore, Geoffrey and the king alone in the court, except for the now-quiet dogs.

"Would the two of you care to return to my chamber? I could use a cup of strong wine."

Leonore saw Geoffrey looking at her quizzically, and spoke for them both. "Yes, Your Majesty, I think that is an excellent idea." She looked expectantly at Geoffrey and he held out his arm as if in a daze. She took it and they followed Liam back up the stairs.

Once in the king's chambers, Geoffrey apparently recovered sufficiently to remember to pour Liam's wine for him. Leonore thought he seemed to be troubled by more than the incident that had just befallen them, but decided to wait until they were alone to question him.

"So tell me exactly what happened," said Liam, and Leonore learned that Geoffrey had overheard Chellasandre and Wallix plotting moments before she had arrived in the court on her way back to her room.

Leonore took over the story at the point when she felt her power return, leaving out the fact that it was much stronger than any power she had felt previously.

"When we spoke earlier, I did not know your power was depleted, Leonore," chided Liam. "How did you get it back so suddenly?"

"I am not sure." The spark of an explanation was beginning to grow in Leonore, but she was not yet ready to share it.

"And what happened to Chellasandre? She seemed quite undone," Liam went on with a chuckle.

"I think that when my magic returned so suddenly, it pushed the spell back into her. It was designed to enchant dogs, not humans. And it was filled with hate. It must have been quite painful to have it all come rushing into her head at once."

"Will she recover?" Liam did not seem overly concerned.

"I am almost sure of it."

Liam nodded, finishing off his wine. He turned to Geoffrey.

"Well, Sir Knight, are you ready to escort Lady Leonore back to her home in the Caernathen wood? She is most eager to return there."

Geoffrey choked on his wine, and King Liam rose and gave him a stout thump between the shoulder blades."

Geoffrey recovered. "I am sorry, but I thought…I thought…"

"What is it, man?" Liam was nonplussed. "Out with it."

"I thought Leonore would be remaining here."

This surprised Leonore. "Wherever did you get that idea, Geoffrey?"

"Earlier. Before the…the thing downstairs," Geoffrey blushed, but went on, "I came up here to see if your meeting was over, and I heard…" He gulped. "I heard you ask Leonore to be your queen!"

"I see." Liam looked solemnly at Geoffrey, then turned his head and winked at Leonore. "And did you not stay long enough to hear the lady refuse me?"

"No, Your Majesty I—" Geoffrey blinked. "Did you say she *refused* you?"

Liam laughed more genuinely. "Yes, Geoffrey, she did." He sighed with mock regret. "Alas, it seems our Lady Leonore is in love with someone else."

* * * * *

The morning was cool and mist rose from the ground as the horses trod quietly on the grassy path through the forest. The leaves, more lush and green than they had been the week before, muffled the sounds of their progress.

Leonore had not slept, but did not feel tired. The surge of power she had felt in the court two nights previous had given her more energy than a child, and had not yet worn off. But she had felt unwilling to speak, except for as required to direct the castle servant to pack her things and to follow Geoffrey's directions.

She knew the knight was confused at her silence, but she had a great puzzle to solve and needed her full concentration to do so. *What was the source of this new power?* It was purer than any she had felt before, and much slower to subside. Colors seemed brighter, smells sharper. The small tendrils of magic she had allowed herself to send out—listening for the emotions of others, communicating with a passing bird—had been more effortless than she would have ever thought possible.

Leonore had quite startled the men on the previous evening, when she had motioned for them to stand back, then ignited the campfire without even a single word of ritual. She had somehow *known* she could do it.

Now as she passed through the familiar environs that would soon lead them into the meadow where they had first met, she considered the only conclusion that made any sense. In the past, the majority of her power had been drawn from that which made her a woman—her sexual being and the gratification of that center. The power had been good and strong, and obtaining it had almost always been pleasurable.

But there had been no sexual contact when this power came. And it had filled her the very moment that Geoffrey had refused to save himself, instead vowing they would die together before he would abandon her to be torn apart by the spell-crazed beasts that surrounded them.

She had admitted in words that she loved Geoffrey, but he had not done the same. Yet, it seemed he must love her as well. And his love was the source from which this new, bright power had sprung.

In all of her years and with all of the men who had renewed her powers, had none of them truly loved her? Many had professed their love and begged her to marry them. But it

Witch's Knight

was the love of smitten youth, not the true love of a man and a woman.

And had she not loved any of them? Yes, she had. And yet Leonore was almost ashamed to admit that her love for them had been more like the way one cares for a beloved pet.

At the moment when it seemed Chellasandre's spell would destroy them both, Leonore had seen a chance to save Geoffrey and had given no thought before telling him to go. And he had refused to do so, instead choosing to protect her.

The conclusion was inescapable. Their mutual love and willingness to die for one another was the source of the power. Their love for one another as equals. And it was immeasurably stronger than the power that came merely from sex.

"It is the meadow!" Horace's excited voice rang out just as Leonore looked up and saw the increased light that heralded the end of the trees. "The enchanted meadow!"

"I hope we will have the chance to enjoy your bathing pools again, Lady Leonore." Wilfred had ridden up beside Leonore and was smiling broadly. "A battered old soldier only gets to behave like a Roman general every so often, and should take advantage of every opportunity."

Leonore smiled in return. "Then let us hasten, Wilfred. The water in the bath is always hot, and the evening is going to be very fine, I think."

Wilfred yipped in glee and slapped the reins against his horse's neck, causing it to leap forward into the grassy meadow. Leonore laughed—the grizzled warrior looked like a youth on his way to a faire.

* * * * *

The cottage was empty but clean. Geoffrey had asked Leonore if a messenger should be sent ahead to Cortlyn and Dunfred, but she had replied that the couple would be preparing for their wedding and should not be troubled.

183

Wilfred and the younger knights had been in the bathing pool since the moment they had fulfilled Geoffrey's requirement that the horses be seen to satisfactorily. After directing Horace to where the soap and honey cleanser could be found, Leonore had hurried to the kitchen croft, saying she would prepare a meal.

Uncertainty gnawed at Geoffrey. There was a great deal he wanted to say to Leonore, but her manner had been distant during the ride.

No, that is not right. Not as if she wants to keep me at a distance. More like she has gone away somewhere and I cannot follow her. Will she come back, I wonder?

Sounds of laughter pulled Geoffrey from his reverie, and he felt a flush of self-consciousness. He had been standing at the intersection of the path to the croft and the walkway that led to the bathing pools. He realized no one had seen him standing as if in a trance, lost in thought. A loud splash made the source of the laughter unmistakable, and gave him at least a temporary direction.

He headed toward the bathing pool, arriving in time to see a naked Wilfred climbing out of the steaming water and onto a large rock. To Geoffrey's increasing amusement, the old man jumped into the water like a peasant boy playing in a cattle pond, tucking up his legs to make the largest possible splash, driving water into Horace's and Morgun's faces.

Wilfred came up for air, water streaming from his head and beard, and Geoffrey laughed aloud, catching the group's attention.

"Sir Geoffrey!" shouted Horace. "Will you not come in? The water is wonderful."

"It does look tempting, but I am afraid of being drowned under waves made by the big hairy bear that has decided to join you this evening."

Wilfred obligingly growled like a bear, to everyone's amusement. "Come on in, sir," he said. "I will promise not to sink you."

"I will hold you to that," said Geoffrey, sitting down to remove his shoes. He froze as a thin sound disturbed the peace of the scene. Geoffrey saw the others had heard it, too. The laughter had left their faces and they held their heads in the unnatural stillness of listening men.

The sound came again, this time discernable as a shout. A female shout, tinged with hysteria. Geoffrey could not make out the words, but the tone of panic was unmistakable. Wilfred and the other men began to clamber toward the sides of the pool, and the shout came again, clear enough to be heard over their slight splashing.

"Lady Leonore!" The shout was now clear. Someone—a woman—was calling out for Leonore. It sounded like it was coming from the cottage now. Geoffrey hurried toward the back door, only to meet Cortlyn as she burst through it.

"Where is the Lady Leonore?" she gasped, winded. Before Geoffrey could answer, Leonore herself appeared and grasped the trembling young woman's hands.

"I am here, Cortlyn. What is it?"

"You must come, Leonore. He will die!"

"Who will die, Cortlyn?" Leonore stared intently into the hysterical woman's face, and Geoffrey could see her begin to calm, no doubt exactly as intended.

"Dunfred," panted Cortlyn, her eyes still bright with panic but no longer darting around frantically. "You must come."

"Of course I will come." Leonore glanced briefly at Geoffrey, and he knew what she wanted.

"Saddle Lady Leonore's horse," he said to Morgun, who already had his braies tied. "Saddle all the horses—we will go with her."

"It was a boar," a slightly calmer Cortlyn was relating. "He went hunting to catch a boar for our wed...wed...wedding feast." Gasps were being overtaken by sobs.

"And was Dunfred gored?" asked Leonore gently.

"Yes." Cortlyn wiped her nose. "Day before yesterday. I thought he was getting better...I made a pack of the herbs just like you taught me. But today..."

"Where is he now?" Leonore.

"At his father's. I did not wish to leave him, but everyone said you were not here and no one would come look. But I thought—"

"Come, Cortlyn." To Geoffrey's surprise, Wilfred, now dressed, put an arm around Cortlyn's shoulders. "The horses will be ready and we can be off. You can ride with me."

Cortlyn looked up at Wilfred's face and Geoffrey could not tell whether she recognized him through her tears, but something in the older man's tone must have comforted her, for she went with him willingly.

"What if he has died while I was gone?" Geoffrey heard her ask, and Wilfred responded in a soothing tone, although the words were not discernable.

Leonore hurried after them, and Geoffrey followed. "Do you need anything, Leonore?"

She glanced back at him and shook her head. "No. If his condition is as dire as I saw in her mind, there will be no time to mix herbs or cast spells. I will have to heal him directly."

Geoffrey almost stopped in his tracks when he realized what Leonore meant to do. *It will be as it was with Wesley.*

He would have to stop her. He could not let her—

Geoffrey's thoughts were interrupted by the sight of Wilfred clambering onto his great horse behind a white-faced Cortlyn. The look in the young girl's eyes as she glanced around and then found Leonore nearly staggered him.

186

Hope and absolute trust. *How can I stop her from doing whatever she must to heal Dunfred? How can I ask her to betray that young girl's trust?*

Seeing he was the last to mount, Geoffrey put his own turmoil aside for the time being, and leapt to his horse. He would decide how he felt about this later. For now, there was a life to save, and there was no time to waste.

Chapter Seventeen

The village of Caernham was larger than Geoffrey had expected, with small, neat houses lining a single street and a few two-story buildings in what must be the exact center. It was still twilight outside, but the inside of the house where Dunfred lay by the fire was already lit with a number of beeswax candles like those Geoffrey had first seen at Leonore's cottage. He remembered her saying that Caernham was noted for its bees. The house smelled strongly of wax and soap, and Geoffrey fleetingly wondered if Dunfred came from a family of chandlers.

Leonore was already kneeling next to the young man, who lay staring on a pallet on the clean wooden floor. His eyes were slightly open but seemed unfocused, and he did not respond to Cortlyn, who was already on his opposite side, squeezing his hand and softly calling his name.

All of the men would have crowded into the small room, had Geoffrey not quickly ascertained the impracticality of this. The room was already almost full—a couple that had to be Dunfred's parents stood nearby, obviously anxious for their son but a little in awe of Leonore. A boy of about fourteen years with Dunfred's square jaw stood at the foot of a ladder, and the faces of younger children peeked from the loft above.

A moan drew Geoffrey's attention back to the wounded man. Leonore had pulled back the blankets and was removing a bandage from Dunfred's thigh. The wound did not look as horrifying as Geoffrey had feared, but he recognized the streaks of red that surrounded it. He had seen similar marks a few days after battles, on the bodies of men wounded with swords or lances. Usually these men died within days of the appearance of the streaks, if not hours, and often these deaths were so horrible that men begged their companions to kill them. Geoffrey shuddered.

Leonore was quiet, her hand held just above the gash, her eyes closed. The room grew silent as all eyes turned to her, and the shuddering breaths that racked the feverish man's chest became painfully audible to all.

Abruptly, Leonore opened her eyes and stood, addressing the room in general.

"He is very weak, but I do not think it is too late. But I must..." her eyes fell on Geoffrey's face, then flickered away toward Cortlyn and the parents. "I must do very strong magic. There is no time for anything else."

"Is it as it was with Wesley?" asked Geoffrey, trying but failing to recapture Leonore's gaze.

"Very much like Wesley."

"I see." Geoffrey felt a wave of jealous nausea rise in his throat, and suppressed it. "And will you heal him in the same way."

Leonore hesitated then spoke. "In much the same way, yes." Finally, she looked directly at Geoffrey, and a moment of silence passed between them. Then, she whirled and again kneeled next to Dunfred and started stripping off his shirt.

"Are you going to...to do it right here in front of everyone?" Geoffrey looked around at the ring of faces in horror.

"There is no time to waste," said Leonore, tearing the sleeve of Dunfred's tunic in her haste. "If anyone does not wish to be affected by the magic they must leave now, but I cannot wait."

Geoffrey felt like bolting from the room, but no one else moved. He saw that Cortlyn was actually *helping* Leonore to remove the rest of Dunfred's clothing. He gulped and waited for Leonore to begin removing her own kirtle, but everyone became very still as Leonore leaned over Dunfred and placed one hand upon his chest and the other, very gently, on the wound.

What is she going to do? Before Geoffrey had the chance to formulate an answer to his wordless question, he felt the hair on his arms and the back of his neck rise. His skin tingled, beginning at his scalp and moving all the way down through his body to his very toes.

"What...?" His voice trailed off as he glanced quickly around the room. Everyone seemed to crackle with energy, and his was not the only hair standing on end. Every face, save his own, was focused intently on what was happening at the side of the hearth, and Geoffrey found his own gaze pulled in the same direction. He would have gasped, but his breath seemed frozen in his chest.

Leonore was glowing. Not like the light that had surrounded her like a mantle when she had confounded the king's mystics on that first meeting. Nor was it the same as the illumination in Wesley's chamber when Leonore held the bedclothes to her face and a light had seemed to shine upon her.

Leonore *shone*. The light did not surround her, it came *from* her. It filled the room with a radiance that illuminated every face, filled every corner and crack of the room. And Dunfred was beginning to shine as well. The light was pure, beautiful and white, yet seemed to contain all the colors of the rainbow.

As Geoffrey gaped, the light began to move and dance and swirl around the room. His chest finally unfroze, and he took in a deep breath that seemed to pull the light into his body. He gasped, and heard others in the room do the same. But he could not pull his eyes away from Leonore and Dunfred.

Geoffrey's ears rang and he at once felt both lightheaded and rooted to the ground as if with iron chains. The tingling in his skin increased, and moved inward to the center of his body. He felt his shaft harden and shudder, and for a moment he thought he would expel his seed like a boy who first feels the desire of a woman's body and cannot control his own response. Moans around the room let him know he was not the only one suddenly in the throes of sexual ecstasy, but no one moved and all eyes remained rapt on Leonore and Dunfred.

As Geoffrey watched, Dunfred's eyes opened. They seemed unfocused, and to roll around the room aimlessly. He groaned, but it did not sound like pain. Geoffrey saw that Dunfred's cock was hard as well, twitching and rising in rhythm with the panting breaths that tore from his chest. Leonore remained motionless, her hands nowhere near Dunfred's eager member, but Dunfred responded as if he were being ridden by a succubus.

"Lady Leonore!" The words were ragged but strong, and Dunfred's eyes were locked on his healer's. Still Leonore did not move or speak.

"Dunfred!" It was Cortlyn's voice that had rent the thickness of the spell, oddly normal in the otherworldly ambience. "Your wound…"

At these words, Geoffrey's focus shifted to the ragged gouge at the top of Dunfred's thigh, only to find it was no longer red and suppurating, and the streaks of dark red and purple that had sprouted from it like the roots of a tree were visibly shrinking and disappearing.

Within moments the rent itself was folding in upon itself, its edges losing their redness and definition, the skin seeming to remake itself. The light continued to swirl, picking up speed as the ringing in Geoffrey's ears reached an almost painful pitch.

"A-a-a-aaah!" Dunfred shrieked aloud as his shaft gave a final convulsion and his seed erupted like a fountain, spraying across his chest, Leonore's hands and the front of Cortlyn's kirtle. Geoffrey felt his cheeks color, and his eyes went to the loft above, but he realized Leonore's body was blocking the view and the younger children could not have seen what had just happened. He felt a horrible urge to giggle and barely managed to stifle it.

He realized the strange pressure in the room was receding and that his skin no longer felt as if lighting raced along his veins. He returned his attention to Leonore and Dunfred, and noticed the glowing light was gone. *When did that happen?*

Dunfred was looking around, blinking in confusion. "Cortlyn? Mother? Lady…"

Leonore was already getting to her feet, wiping her hands on a piece of fabric that had appeared from somewhere. "Welcome back, Dunfred."

Dunfred would have risen, but Cortlyn held him down and began pulling the quilt around his nakedness. After fervent but brief thanks to Leonore, Dunfred's parents were soon also gathered close to him. The children in the loft were scrambling down the ladder and the people who had been lingering in the open doorway began to push in. Within moments the room was stifling, and Geoffrey began pushing his way through the boisterous crowd in the direction of the door.

Leonore appeared to be trying to do the same, but was further hampered by the congratulations, thanks and even obeisance from the onlookers. She smiled and spoke with each person who accosted her, but when she glanced up, Geoffrey caught her eye and read her expression plainly. *Help me,* her face seemed to say. Geoffrey changed directions and came to her elbow. He raised his voice over the exclamations and laughter of the crowd.

"The Lady Leonore needs to breathe," he said, taking her firmly by the elbow. "Please let her pass."

Instantly, the crowd parted and let Geoffrey and Leonore through.

"Thank you," she said fervently, as soon as they were through the door and into the cool evening air. "I seldom come to town openly. I love the villagers but they can be a little overwhelming."

"Actually, I would probably still be stuck in there had I not used the excuse of escorting you to make my escape." Geoffrey released Leonore's arm with reluctance. He had felt her power still thrumming in her veins the moment he touched her, and the sensation had been surprisingly soothing. He had not wanted to let go.

"Perhaps we should leave before anyone thinks to look for us," suggested Leonore, and Geoffrey was relieved to hear her suggest what he had wanted to say. He signaled to the other knights, and within moments the horses were ready for their much slower return through the small breadth of wood between the village and the vale that concealed Leonore's cottage.

Geoffrey had many questions for Leonore, but he held his tongue on the return journey. He wanted to ponder what he had seen, and Leonore did not seem eager to discuss the matter with him.

After dismounting and passing their horses to Horace and Morgun, Leonore stopped briefly and turned to Geoffrey on the path leading to the back of the cottage.

"I noticed the wet hair on the other men when we left for the village," she said. "You did not then have the opportunity to bathe before we left?"

"I was just about to when Cortlyn arrived."

Leonore nodded. "In that case, I wonder if you would consider sharing a bath with me? I think there is much to be said between us, Geoffrey. I am ready to speak if you are ready to listen."

Geoffrey was surprised, but the thought of slipping naked into a pool of steaming water with Leonore sent a shudder along his skin and caused a sudden tightness in his groin. "I would be most pleased, Leonore."

She nodded. "Very well. I will be along in a few moments. Perhaps you can persuade Wilfred and the men to retire early."

So, she wants privacy. The pressure in his braies increased, and Geoffrey nodded. "I am sure I can," he replied, as Leonore nodded a second time before disappearing through the cottage's back door.

* * * * *

Geoffrey was already seated in the pool as Leonore approached. She wore only a robe of the most gossamer silk, which had come from far to the south and would be unrecognized even by those who sewed for the wealthiest women in these environs.

Leonore had chosen the robe because she wanted to be beautiful for Geoffrey, but now she was considering she may have made a mistake. She wanted to make love with him— very much so—but she had a great deal to tell him first. The feel of the slippery fabric rubbing against her nipples, along with the knowledge that she would soon be sharing a bath with a very naked Geoffrey, was making her desire flame so hotly that she feared she would not be able to wait.

Geoffrey's face turned and Leonore saw an expression of shock, then pleasure, followed by desire. She knew the moonlight shone upon the floating folds of fabric and outlined her form, making her look ethereal and enchanting, which was what the garment had been designed for.

"Thank you for waiting for me, Sir Geoffrey. Are the men...?"

"They have gone to their beds. Although Wilfred did not look well pleased."

"Excellent." Leonore drank up Geoffrey's scrutiny. His eyes looked very dark in the moonlight, and she felt her nipples harden and an ache start at her belly and move between her legs. *Not yet. There is plenty of time.*

194

She briefly considered concealing herself with the drying cloth she carried, but instead simply slipped the robe off her shoulders and sank gracefully into the pool, swiftly but without haste. Seated opposite Geoffrey, both of them up to their necks in water, she immediately felt more able to concentrate on the task at hand, even if there was less actually separating them than a moment before.

"Geoffrey..." Having planned a number of things she wanted to say, Leonore realized she had not planned a logical place to start. She decided on a different strategy. "I think you have questions to ask me."

Geoffrey sighed. "Yes. Many. I hardly know where to start."

Leonore heard her own laughter peal softly in the night air. "Then it seems we are of the same mind, Geoffrey. So much has passed between us in so short a time. And although I have lived longer than I care to admit, much of it has been entirely new to me. So I thought that by letting you ask the questions, I would know how to begin."

Geoffrey chuckled as well. "In that case, Leonore, I will start at the end. What happened tonight? I thought you would...when you said that Dunfred's condition was like Wesley's when you...healed him, I thought that meant..."

Leonore could see that Geoffrey was struggling with words that made him uncomfortable, but decided not to help him. *Let him say it aloud. It will be better if he is the one.*

"I thought you would have to lay your naked body against his in order to heal him. And then when you did not..." Geoffrey shook his head. "Then I wondered if I had been wrong about Wesley."

"No." Leonore wanted no misunderstanding. "In the past, the only way I could channel that much magic that quickly, I always had to have as much physical contact with the subject as possible. Skin to skin. With a man, it has sometimes even been necessary to have his member inside me."

"Then why was it not so tonight?" To Leonore's relief, Geoffrey's voice held no tinge of jealousy, only honest curiosity. She considered her answer.

"Tonight I just knew that I could do it without the sexual contact." She considered her next words carefully. In the past few days of self-examination and contemplation, she had already formed the conclusion. But this was the first time she would put it into words.

"My magic has become stronger. Much stronger. And its nature has changed."

"Changed how? And when did you renew it? We have not...you have not..."

"I have not coupled with anyone," Leonore finished for him. "No. But I did renew my magic. Actually, *you* renewed it, Geoffrey."

"When? How?"

"In the court at the castle. When you would have sacrificed yourself to save me."

Geoffrey looked confused. "I do not understand."

"Neither did I. It had never happened before." Leonore took a deep breath and finished the rest of it. "When each of us chose the life of the other before our own, right at the same moment, I was renewed by *love*. It was a hundred times, maybe a thousand times stronger than the power I have drawn from sexual gratification. And it lasts longer."

Leonore moved across the pool to be closer to Geoffrey. She reached below the surface of the water and took his hands in hers, pulling them out of the water to hold them in the moonlight. "I love you, Geoffrey. And you love me."

Geoffrey was silent, gazing into her eyes. Leonore waited. She did not need him to tell her he loved her. But she *wanted* him to acknowledge that what she said was true. Finally, he spoke.

"I never understood why I was always so *angry* with you." Geoffrey's smile was sheepish. "I told myself it was none of my affair if you shared you bed with a thousand men. It had nothing to do with me."

"And I never understood why I cared that you were angry." Leonore's smile matched Geoffrey's. "Now I know."

"Now we both know. I love you, Leonore."

At Geoffrey's words, a sensation began in Leonore's center—a feeling at one time new and familiar. She lowered their clasped hands and held them against her belly.

"The power is rising, Geoffrey. It is the same as on that day in the court. I am being filled with our love!"

Geoffrey's eyes were full of a combination of wonder and desire. "It is a fine thing that our love can renew your power, Leonore. But a part of me is saddened that you can no longer replenish your magic through sex."

"I think I know what part you are speaking of." Leonore reached for his shaft. It was hardening, as she had expected. "But Geoffrey, I said that to draw power from sex was no longer *necessary*. I did not say it was not *possible*." She heard him gasp as she wrapped her fingers around him. "Actually, I have been wondering what it would feel like to fill myself with both types of power at the same time. I do not know if it can be done."

Geoffrey's smile grew wicked. "Well, I suppose there is only one way to find out."

"On the contrary, Sir Geoffrey. I can think of any number of ways!"

The new power, the one Leonore had already started to think of as the Light of Love, was already pulsing in her veins. "I want you to feel everything I feel, Geoffrey. Not just what our bodies are doing, but what our hearts are feeling. I think I can…*we* can make that happen. Will you try with me?"

"I will." Geoffrey's voice was a hoarse whisper. "But I do not think I can wait much longer."

"Nor can I." Maintaining the light pressure of her hand on his cock, Leonore used her other hand to bring Geoffrey's fingers between her legs. "Feel me, Geoffrey. I am slick with desire for you, even under the water." She shuddered as his probing proved her words to be true.

Leonore felt the old magic, the familiar friend of many years, bubble to the surface like a warm spring breaking through the earth. She heard Geoffrey gasp, and looked at his face. His eyes were shining.

"Can you feel it, Geoffrey? The magic?"

"Yes. It is astonishing. And I can feel my fingers inside your body. I mean, the way you feel it."

"Kiss me."

Geoffrey needed no prodding. His mouth found hers, hungry and sweet. A vortex seemed to open beneath them, a vortex of the bright, shining Light of Love. They were pulled into it, and even while their tongues intertwined and tasted, Leonore moaned as she suddenly perceived Geoffrey's senses—the soft pressure on his throbbing shaft and the slippery tightness against his fingers as they explored more deeply into her body.

At the same time, she felt the warming caress of the Light of Love as it circled them, tugged at them, infused them. A groan from Geoffrey told her he was experiencing her sensations as well. His thumb found the tiny bud at the opening of her core, and he squeezed it lightly. Leonore jerked upright as a flash of pleasure shot through her limbs, and she would have screamed had her mouth not still been locked with Geoffrey's.

Geoffrey stiffened as well, and drew back from the kiss. "I did not know...I had no idea! Let me try that again." He ran the end of his finger over the nub of flesh, and his body stiffened at the same time as Leonore's. He laughed like a child.

"I want to feel everything. I want to touch every part of your body and feel what you feel." Leonore did not argue, especially when he again took the bud between his fingers and squeezed gently. "Aaaaah." He writhed a little, as if it was his own body being teased.

Geoffrey put his hand on Leonore's, stilling the strokes against his cock. "You must stop that for now. It will make me finish too soon, and I want to...to try some things."

Understanding, Leonore released his shaft and lay back in the water. She placed her hands behind her head and smiled. "Go ahead, Sir Knight. Try all of your experiments. But keep in mind I have a list of my own, and I intend to have my way as soon as you give me a turn."

"We must get out of this pool. I want to see what I am doing."

Leonore did not hesitate to agree.

Chapter Eighteen

๙

The moon, waxing over the nine days since Geoffrey had first stood and seen this pool, had finally grown full and yellow. The soft, padded quilt Leonore had produced—he did not want to ask why it was kept so conveniently near the pools—framed her body, which shone like a polished white stone in the golden light. The night was so bright he could see the green in her eyes and the copper glinting in her hair.

I can feel what she feels. Every emotion, every sensation. And she can experience what I feel as well. This, thought Geoffrey, *could be the longest and best night of my life.*

First and foremost, he felt Leonore's desire. Even now, not touching her, he could feel the tingles of anticipation that raced through her body and caused her to contract in spasms of delicious expectation.

"How do you want to start?" she asked huskily.

He ran his eyes down her body, trying to imagine what it would feel like—to her—for him to touch each part of it.

"Slowly, I think." He lay next to her and buried his face in her hair, which was wet at the tips and smelled delightfully of the honey soap she used to wash it. His gaze was captured by her perfect ear, so he reached over and brushed it with his lips, then explored it with his tongue. He saw the silky hairs on her arms stand up as he felt the answering shiver run along the back of his own neck. He moved his lips to her throat, tracing his tongue along the line of her jaw.

"Geoffrey." He heard Leonore's whisper in his ear, but felt the impulse that caused her to say it within his own mind, his own heart.

"Yes, my love?" he replied, but he already knew what she wanted. Her entire body pulsed with the desire for him to touch her everywhere at once, and he almost vibrated as the need coursed through his own veins.

"Touch me. Please...just touch me." Even as she made her request, Geoffrey moved his lips and hands lower on her body, kissing the hollow at the base of her throat as his fingers found her breasts.

Leonore shuddered as he squeezed the mounds of flesh, and he felt the pleasure at the exact moment he knew she wanted him—needed him—to grasp them more firmly and more urgently. He was happy to oblige.

"Take them—" Leonore began then stopped as her gasp cut off her words.

"In my mouth?" finished Geoffrey. "Between my teeth?" Even as she groaned her assent, his lips found her hardened nipples, and he shivered at the fine line between pleasure and pain as his tongue and teeth explored the heightened sensitivity that was the product of her arousal. He nipped them, and felt his own body jump in concert with her response.

The colossal surge of desire that spread through her loins—and thus through his—caused him to throw his head back in astonishment. Was a woman's need always so strong, so insistent?

"Geoffrey," Leonore panted. "My...your cock..."

For a moment, Geoffrey was puzzled. Then, the sensations coming from his own body blazed to the surface, and he realized he had been ignoring his own feelings in the wonder of experiencing Leonore's desire. While he was doing so, his member had continued to react of its own accord. His shaft was so hard, he felt as if he could cut through glass with its head, and it throbbed with more intensity than he had ever felt before.

"Let me…I must…" Leonore's words were almost unintelligible, but he knew — *felt* — what she was asking, and he obeyed. Shifting his weight, he placed the head of his cock against the wet — oh-so very wet — opening where her eager hands grasped and led it. Within less than a moment, he was buried within the fiery furnace of her body.

"Not yet…it is too soon," he protested, but they could no more stop the inevitable than they could prevent the rising of the moon. Deep, deep within her, they found a rhythm that was older than time and as new as this unbelievable, perfect night.

As the simultaneous waves of their orgasms began to rise, Leonore threw her head back and screamed. For a moment, Geoffrey could not tell if the sound came from his own throat or from hers, then realized it hardly mattered. It seemed as if they did not even exist as separate entities, but were two halves of a single, primal beast. He added his howls to hers, and did not care who heard them.

* * * * *

She is so beautiful when she sleeps. Even as the thought came, Geoffrey grinned. He found her just as beautiful when awake, but the sight of her coppery curls spread across the linen in the moon and starlight that streamed through the window almost stopped his heart.

She loves me. This made him smile again. He knew Leonore's pledge of love was true and honest. He had *felt* her emotions. She had also said she believed the magical bond between them would mean they would always be able to know one another's emotions, at least when they were together.

And they would be together. Geoffrey had much to tell Leonore. He had meant to tell her on this night, but every time they started to converse, their bodies conspired to lead to another kind of intercourse. That was as well. He had plenty of time to tell her.

As he settled himself more comfortably on the pillows, he recalled the meeting he had with the king before they left, when Leonore was saying her goodbyes to her servant and instructing the cook in the use of the herbs she was leaving behind.

"Morgun is ready to take over his estate, I think. I told him I would reward him on his twenty-first birthday, should he merit it."

"I agree, Liam. He has matured much these last weeks."

"I have been thinking of giving him Westwold," said Liam, giving Geoffrey a speculative glace.

"But that is my—" Geoffrey started to interrupt, but the king raised a hand.

"Yes, and you have done a fine job with it. But I thought you might like something larger. I need someone I can trust with some of my more remote holdings. For example…"

Liam's expression was inscrutable. "Caernham has long been without a Lord. It is a rich land, and they have sent their tithes regularly, but I think they could prosper even more under the right leadership."

Geoffrey had been silent, wondering at the king's intent. Liam had gone on.

"After you take Leonore home, take some time to look around the village and the outlying farms. They send me the most extraordinary honey and candles, you know. If you decide to stay, you can send me a message with Wilfred."

Now, gazing at a sleeping Leonore, he knew he did not have to look further. He had already made up his mind.

As if she sensed his regard, Leonore stirred and opened one grass-green eye. "Good morning, Sir Knight."

"It is not yet morning, Leonore."

"And yet you look wide awake." Looking at him more closely, she frowned. "Is there something troubling you, Geoffrey?"

"No. But there is something I would tell you."

Leonore stretched, and the bed coverings slipped down to reveal one milky breast, its nipple rosy from his earlier attentions. Geoffrey was surprised to feel his member stir in response. It had already been well used this night.

He caught Leonore's grin, and he knew she had felt his cock stiffen. Indeed, he could also feel her response, as her nipple tingled and grew erect under his regard. Feeling his own ardor grow in concert with hers, he reached for her.

"Was there not something you wished to discuss?" Leonore asked, as Geoffrey took her in his arms.

"Later, my love. We have all the time in the world."

The End

Why an electronic book?

We live in the Information Age — an exciting time in the history of human civilization, in which technology rules supreme and continues to progress in leaps and bounds every minute of every day. For a multitude of reasons, more and more avid literary fans are opting to purchase e-books instead of paper books. The question from those not yet initiated into the world of electronic reading is simply: *Why?*

1. *Price.* An electronic title at Ellora's Cave Publishing and Cerridwen Press runs anywhere from 40% to 75% less than the cover price of the exact same title in paperback format. Why? Basic mathematics and cost. It is less expensive to publish an e-book (no paper and printing, no warehousing and shipping) than it is to publish a paperback, so the savings are passed along to the consumer.

2. *Space.* Running out of room in your house for your books? That is one worry you will never have with electronic books. For a low one-time cost, you can purchase a handheld device specifically designed for e-reading. Many e-readers have large, convenient screens for viewing. Better yet, hundreds of titles can be stored within your new library — on a single microchip. There are a variety of e-readers from different manufacturers. You can also read e-books on your PC or laptop computer. (Please note that Ellora's Cave does not endorse any specific brands.

You can check our websites at www.ellorascave.com or www.cerridwenpress.com for information we make available to new consumers.)

3. *Mobility.* Because your new e-library consists of only a microchip within a small, easily transportable e-reader, your entire cache of books can be taken with you wherever you go.

4. *Personal Viewing Preferences.* Are the words you are currently reading too small? Too large? Too… ANNOYING? Paperback books cannot be modified according to personal preferences, but e-books can.

5. *Instant Gratification.* Is it the middle of the night and all the bookstores near you are closed? Are you tired of waiting days, sometimes weeks, for bookstores to ship the novels you bought? Ellora's Cave Publishing sells instantaneous downloads twenty-four hours a day, seven days a week, every day of the year. Our webstore is never closed. Our e-book delivery system is 100% automated, meaning your order is filled as soon as you pay for it.

Those are a few of the top reasons why electronic books are replacing paperbacks for many avid readers.

As always, Ellora's Cave and Cerridwen Press welcome your questions and comments. We invite you to email us at Comments@ellorascave.com or write to us directly at Ellora's Cave Publishing Inc., 1056 Home Avenue, Akron, OH 44310-3502.

erridwen, the Celtic Goddess of wisdom, was the muse who brought inspiration to storytellers and those in the creative arts. Cerridwen Press encompasses the best and most innovative stories in all genres of today's fiction. Visit our site and discover the newest titles by talented authors who still get inspired - much like the ancient storytellers did, once upon a time.

Cerridwen Press

www.cerridwenpress.com

*Discover for yourself why readers can't get enough
of the multiple award-winning publisher*
Ellora's Cave.
*Whether you prefer e-books or paperbacks,
be sure to visit EC on the web at
www.ellorascave.com
for an erotic reading experience that will leave you
breathless.*